# "LADIES AND GENTLEMEN, THE PRESIDENT OF THE UNITED STATES . . ."

*"My fellow Americans. This morning, men's souls were seared by the butchery which has taken place at the site of the United Nations.*

*"Bloated with madness and blinded by a paranoiac craving for vengeance, a foreign government struck a terrible, bloody blow against innocent people of all nations . . . all nations except one.*

*"I accuse the State of Israel and its agents in America of perpetrating this horrendous crime! And I have the evidence to prove it!"*

●

The President's speech immediately provoked riots and bloody rampages around the world.

Because that was the plan.

Because the President's speech has been written *before* the fact.

Because the President was a Nazi.

NEMESIS

# NEMESIS

## PHIL DAVIS

AVON
PUBLISHERS OF BARD, CAMELOT AND DISCUS BOOKS

NEMESIS is an original publication of Avon Books. This work
has never before appeared in book form.


AVON BOOKS
A division of
The Hearst Corporation
959 Eighth Avenue
New York, New York 10019

First Avon Printing, June, 1979

AVON TRADEMARK REG. U.S. PAT. OFF. AND IN
OTHER COUNTRIES, MARCA REGISTRADA, HECHO EN
U.S.A.

Printed in the U.S.A.

For my wife
IDA
And my son
DAVID
without their faith
and encouragement
this book would never
have been written

# Preface

## Damascus, Syria

"Are you all right?" The defense counsel peered at him anxiously.

David nodded, but his eyes clouded as he thought of the incredible events that had led to this predicament that confronted not only him but the entire world with terrible consequences. *How could God have allowed it to happen!*

Why?

David closed his eyes and mouthed: *"Kee ayl gadol Adonai u-melekh gadol al kol Elohim."* For the Lord is a great God and a great King above all Gods.

He shuddered and switched his thoughts to Myrna. She would come in time. The plot and the plotters would be exposed. The world would be restored to sanity.

But what if something happened to Myrna? What if they stopped her? And she could not get through to him?

"*Gamoor,*" he said under his breath in Hebrew. *Finished.*

The defense counsel read his thoughts. "She'll be here."

"I know," murmured David, but he wasn't sure. The message was clear that she was on her way, but there were too many variables. Time, mainly. Time and the organization and the powerful force of hate. A vicious combination for one woman to take on.

He looked about the great hall. Byzantine. Mosaic incrustation in the wood. The walls veneered with marble. Ancient. Breathtakingly beautiful. For him a magnificent torture chamber.

Was it to end here? On the Sabbath?

David raised his eyes to the center dome and beyond. Silently he mouthed the Kaddish. For himself.

The dais directly in front of him rose to an imposing height. Behind it were seven tall-backed chairs from which the seven justices would issue their blight. He expected nothing less. Unless Myrna arrived in time.

He turned to his defense counsel. "Will they let me speak?"

"Yes."

"For how long?"

"As long as . . ." He paused, then spread his hands as if to indicate there was no limit.

"I'll need twelve hours," said David. "Maybe more. There's a lot to tell. No matter what happens to me I want the world to hear every detail. From the beginning. Some will believe me. Just a seed. And in time the truth will bloom." His face grew sad. "That's if Myrna doesn't come."

The defense counsel nodded his assurance. "Myrna will come," he said. "Then it will be over."

Strung along the back of the chamber were the television cameras of all nations with their crews waiting.

On a platform above the cameras the foreign interpreters were chattering in unison into microphones, preparing their respective nations for this, the most special of events.

Above them were the foreign correspondents at their telephones.

At one side sat the chief executives of many nations. Including representatives of the United States. Never before in man's history had there been a proceeding like this.

Silently, the spectators filed into the vast chamber. When it was full, the massive doors boomed shut and the armed guards took their assigned positions.

David looked up at the dais and watched the seven judges take their seats.

"Since this trial is unprecedented," intoned the chief justice, "and will be viewed by millions around the world, it will be conducted in English. The formalities and the rigid rules of evidence will be dispensed with in order to grant the defendant every possible advantage.

"Let the record show, according to our laws, the defendant is presumed to be innocent."

A mutter rose from the assemblage.

The chief justice brought his gavel down three times and the chamber grew silent. He went on. "Therefore, it becomes the duty of the attorney general to introduce sufficient evidence to dissipate the presumption of innocence."

He gazed down from his height and ordered that the trial begin.

# PART ONE

# 1

## New York City
## Friday

Harry Riordon stood in the rear of the visitor's gallery of the United Nations and shook his head in disbelief at the way the vote was going. Surely the coming evil was obvious. Yet where were the voices raised against it?

The United States abstained. The gallery booed.

Harry wondered, why not a forceful stand against honoring a notorious murderer? Abstention—a coward's way of approval.

They were establishing a precedent for the righteousness of terror.

"*Da!*" bellowed the delegate from the Soviet Union. It reverberated through the hall like thunder.

The Arabs laughed.

Great Britain: "In favor!"
France: "In favor!"
Sweden, Mexico, West Germany: "In favor!"
The Netherlands: "Against!" A beacon.

The Israeli delegation stared hypnotically at the electronic board registering the votes. Each flick of the lights giving the lie to the illusion that these nations were ever united in justice.

Harry backed out of one of the exit doors and hurried away to make his report.

Outside, in the April sunshine, a flock of pigeons wheeled in front of the U.N. Building, then as if at a signal, plunged in formation toward U.N. Plaza, their reflection flickering in the glass siding of the tall rectangle.

They swooped within three feet of the pavement, and took off without landing, their wings beating noisily at the air as they gained altitude. They headed southwest from whence they had come.

For the past two weeks the exercise had been performed to perfection.

The training had been going on for six months.

No one seemed to notice.

Julius Lipman, well-tailored in a glen plaid suit despite his somewhat paunchy, middle-aged physique, left the Fifth Avenue branch of the Bank of New York with half a million dollars in his attaché case. He didn't think the man would need it. But it had to be presented.

He stepped into the waiting Continental and was driven to the David Ring Building on the corner of Third Avenue and Fifty-fourth Street where he was met by an armed guard.

Together they entered the busy lobby, striding past the bank of elevators operated manually by uniformed

8

retired enforcement officers. All armed. Security for the entire building; the nerve center of Ring Enterprises.

The guard at the information booth made note of the time of Lipman's arrival; his gaze followed them to the penthouse elevator.

The elevator door, fashioned in hammered, burnished copper, bore the imprint of the Tablet on which were engraved the Commandments in Hebrew. Handwrought by David Ring. Symbolic of David Ring.

Lipman inserted a laminated code card in a slot beside the door and it slid open. The guard stationed himself outside. It was his regular post.

The elevator rose swiftly to the penthouse foyer where the walls were graced by Chagalls and Picassos. Pedestals sustained works of sculpture by Epstein, Lipchitz, Moore.

A tin mezuzah was tacked onto a doorjamb.

Directly ahead was the sitting room; but Lipman strode toward a corridor that led to the gymnasium.

As he entered, he heard the sounds of bodily contact mingled with assorted grunts. It was apparent that a contest of some kind was in progress, but the action was shielded by the presence of a half dozen onlookers.

Lipman scanned the area for a moment, then spied Yoshio Murakami seated at a small table on which rested an attaché case the same size as his own.

Murakami rose as Lipman approached. They bowed silently, then exchanged attaché cases and flipped them open to examine the contents.

"A half million," said Lipman. "Correct, Mr. Murakami?"

"That is correct, Mr. Lipman."

Lipman snapped the case shut while Murakami began to count the packets of bills in the case handed him. He paused to look curiously at Lipman, who was calmly loading his pipe.

"Are you not going to count?" he asked.

"What for?" said Lipman coldly, touching a match to the pipe's bowl.

"To make certain the amount I gave you is correct."

"If Mr. Ring loses the match then it wouldn't matter, even if what you handed me was counterfeit, would it?"

"But if Mr. Ring wins, then—"

"If he wins," interrupted Lipman, "then you can't afford to be short."

The logic struck home. Also the implied threat. "My apologies." Murakami snapped the case shut.

Lipman removed a document from his inside pocket and handed it to Murakami. "Assumption-of-risk agreement. I've already signed it on behalf of Mr. Ring."

Murakami examined it perfunctorily, then applied his signature. Together they crossed the arena to witness the match.

It was a combination kung fu-Karate bout between a huge black-belted Japanese and the tall, lean David Ring.

Six Japanese gentlemen in business suits stood watching without a show of emotion.

A doctor viewed the match from the other side of the mat, watching carefully for a blow that might prove fatal.

No referee; no scoring of points. The match could end only by a permanent crippling or surrender . . . or death.

The combatants circled, eyeing each other warily. David seemed tired, breathing heavily; the Japanese, fresh.

Suddenly, the Japanese executed a series of hand thrusts and kicks that seemed to catch David off guard and he went down with a sickening crunch. He lay still.

The audience leaned forward tensely.

A sharp intake of breath from Murakami.

Lipman's face, impassive.

The Japanese leaped high, and with a blood-curdling scream came crashing down toward David's head.

It wasn't there. David rolled away, scrambling to his feet. But his right arm appeared useless. It hung limply at his side; from all appearances broken. His face was contorted in pain.

The Japanese stalked. Again and again he struck the dangling arm. David staggered under the impact of each blow and cried out in pain.

Too obvious?

Not to the Japanese. With a cry of victory he lunged for the kill. But in a flash the seemingly crippled arm lashed up and the side of the hand cut across the man's throat.

For an instant there was a look of surprise on the Oriental's face. Then with a convulsive gasp for breath he fell over on his back, clutching at his throat, his mouth open, his body flopping like a beached fish.

David signaled the doctor. "Do a tracheotomy," he said. "Otherwise he doesn't have much time."

"Congratulations, Mr. Ring," said Murakami. He handed the attaché case to Lipman.

David bowed. He wasn't even breathing hard. "Let this be evidence that there is no such thing as a superior race as you had boasted. Just superior training, sir." He turned to Lipman. "Deposit it in the hospital fund."

The doctor was tending the man on the floor. The

six onlookers eyed David with awe. He had just defeated the champion of the world.

"Gentlemen," said David. "Let me remind you that according to our agreement, your terrorist group is to be disbanded and a notice to that effect is to be published in all major Japanese newspapers."

The men bowed and an attendant escorted them away while the doctor called down to the hospital for a stretcher for the wounded gladiator.

David walked with measured steps to the swimming pool. He stood at the water's edge, his body trembling as if in the throes of a malaria attack. The aftereffect of the match. It shouldn't have been that close. He'd underestimated his opponent. It would never happen again.

A deep breath. He held it until his body regained its control. Then he raised his head and cried, *"Sh'ma Yisrael, Adonai Elohaynu, Adonai Ehad!"*

He dove into the pool and with swift, sure strokes covered two laps before he turned on his back and glided leisurely, his eyes closed, his breath slow and steady. He thought of the agreement with the Japanese. Would they adhere to it? What if they did not? The cells in Tokyo knew of the contract. If the group reneged they'd be held up to ridicule. They could not afford to lose face.

Harry Riordon came in quietly and sat down. David waved him a welcome. Riordon was a tightly knit Irishman of medium build with a head of thick dark red hair and a freckled florid complexion.

"I just came from the U.N., David," said Harry. "They voted to allow Yassim Sivad to address the General Assembly."

David's eyes clouded. "I was afraid of that. It gives them a sense of legitimacy. When is he due?"

"Next Friday. A week from today. I think we should try to stop him."

"Why?"

"There could be trouble."

"For me?"

"Of course."

"I've lived with trouble."

"This is different."

David thought a moment, moving his arms languidly to stay afloat; then buried himself in the water and swam beneath the surface for two minutes. When he came up he barely gasped for air. "Why is this trouble different?" he asked.

"Just a hunch. You've been giving that Arab bunch of hoodlums a bad time with your eye-for-an-eye treatment. I think Sivad's presence has more significance than just an ego trip. He knows you'll be a stone's throw away. He's never been this close to you. He'll arrive with an entourage that could spell out a lot of things. Kamikaze stuff, you know?" He shrugged. "Like I said, it's only a hunch."

David climbed out of the pool, water cascading from his muscular physique, and wrapped himself in terry cloth. An attendant appeared with a bowl of fruit.

"We deal in facts, Harry," said David. "Facts and talent." He reclined on a lounge and began peeling an orange. "Our enterprises cover half the earth. We did it with facts and talent, not hunches." He nodded toward the arena. "You didn't ask how we made out with Murakami's man."

Harry grinned. There was something about Harry, a sadness that belied the twinkle in his green eyes. "I never question talent, David," he said.

"We might have lost."

"You wouldn't have been here to tell me about it."

13

"I wasn't on my best game." He shivered slightly. "Anyway, I think we've put an end to the Japanese terrorists." He munched a segment of orange in silence for a moment, savoring its flavor. A wistful expression crossed his gaunt, Semitic features. "If only there was a way to deal with Sivad," he murmured. "As you would with an honorable man. Or a greedy one."

"Stop him," said Harry.

"How?"

"I don't know. Bottle him up somewhere, maybe. I don't know."

David began disposing of the orange in earnest while his mind meandered in search of an answer to Harry's hunch.

He came up empty.

"We have seven days," said Harry helpfully. "We should be able to dream up some ideas in seven days."

David shook his head. "Bad timing, Harry. We should have acted long before the fact. We knew Sivad's appearance was on the U.N. agenda. We could have tried to mobilize our skills to influence the voting. We did nothing. Sivad will be here legally. If as a result I'll be in some kind of jeopardy . . ." He smiled. "I've been there before. But I respect your hunch, Harry. Tell Lippy about it. He might have some thoughts."

Harry rose. "See you at the meeting." He walked away quickly.

He was a complex man, Harry Riordon. David's age—thirty-eight. Irish Catholic, studied for the priesthood, ordained, then resigned shortly after. Because of disagreement with the hierarchy.

A free spirit. Totally involved with David out of friendship and a loyalty that began during childhood.

He took no special interest in David's Jewishness. It was what he stood for that gave Harry his zest for

14

living. Had he not rediscovered David after a ten-year separation he would have found life too oppressive to bear.

Thoughts of the implications of Sivad's visit gnawed at his guts. He feared David was taking it too lightly.

He would press it at the meeting.

He sought out Lipman.

# 2

## New York City, Kennedy International Airport Friday

The Lufthansa 747 approached the space assigned to it. Inside, Klaus Wagner, a blond, powerfully built German, prepared to disembark. He carried a single, well-packed flight bag and a raincoat. Nothing else. Except a hate. That and a kind of frenetic exhilaration.

In the customs area, behind one of the counters, Carl Fredericks, a thin, tense man in a trenchcoat, showed the customs officer his FBI identification, then stood scanning the human jumble for a face.

Klaus Wagner paused in the entrance, searching, waiting. Better to stay where he was, he thought. He placed his flight bag at his feet and lit a cigarette.

Fredericks spotted him.

Wagner saw him picking his way toward him. He grinned.

The beginning.

As they strode along the terminal concourse, the following conversation took place.

FREDERICKS: *Sie müssen sich gut überlegen, wie Sie das Geld gebrauchen wollen, wenn Sie Erfolg haben möchten.*

WAGNER: *Wir werden Erfolg haben, vorausgesetzt. Tunnen Sie das Ihrige.*

FREDERICKS: *Natürlich. Unsere Organisation ist sehr einflussreich.*

WAGNER: *Sie wissen doch, dass wir planten David Ring vor Gericht zu stellen.*

FREDERICKS: *Ja, das wird das Meisterstück sein.*

They emerged from the terminal and entered the black Mercedes that was parked at the curb. The chauffeur drove off without receiving any instructions.

## Lake George, N.Y.
## Friday

Four cars, a single passenger in each, pulled off a secluded country road and stopped in front of an iron gate that guarded a driveway lined with thick shrubbery. The driver of the lead car aimed an electronic device at the gate and .it swung open.

The cars moved slowly until they reached an area cleared for parking.

In the background, the lake shimmered in the afternoon sun. The sounds of water lapping at the sandy beach could be heard.

Near the parking area, Anna Thornton stood on the

porch of her country mansion waiting to greet her guests.

She was a strikingly attractive woman. Dark-haired, thirtyish and statuesque. Her hair was pulled back in a severe bun in recognition of the seriousness of the occasion.

Reverend Carson was the first to reach her.

Then came General Marley. U.S. Army, Retired.

Followed by Secretary of State Brandon.

Senator Franklyn brought up the rear.

After the preliminary amenities, Anna ushered them inside.

A half hour later, the black Mercedes with Fredericks and Wagner drove up.

The driver pulled into the parking area and Wagner and Fredericks got out.

Wagner looked about him. A gentle, summery breeze stirred the limbs of the pines. The air was clean with a freshness free of pollution. Klaus Wagner murmured: "Here we will make history."

# 3

## New York City
## Friday

The group sat around the conference room in the penthouse of the David Ring Building waiting for David to show up for the regular Friday meeting.

Present were:

Lipman, comptroller; pipe-smoking; pallid complexion; thinning, light-brown hair; something distracted about him.

Harry Riordon, investigator; sad eyes brooding; large, freckled hands folded on the table before him.

Jonathan Hayes, Harry's partner; a black man; hard-muscled; knew the harsh bite of prejudice as malevolent as that by which the Jews were afflicted.

Alfred Michaels, secret operative; balding; nondescript but with a toughness that brooked no nonsense from anyone.

Myrna Lu, researcher; small, dark-haired master of the martial arts; amazing agility and power packed into her compact body.

These were David's childhood playmates.

Still David's playmates.

Only the games were different.

David came in briskly and joined the group at the round table. There was no exchange of amenities. He plunged in with: "About Yassim Sivad's visit to the United Nations next week. Pretty ugly. Gives you an idea of the world balance. Harry thinks it could spell trouble for me. What's more important—what does it mean that the United States abstained during the roll call? What do you think, Lippy?"

Lippy began filling his pipe. "Harry and I discussed it. I don't see any real trouble. Just a dark brown taste." He flicked his lighter at the packed bowl and puffed hard, drawing in the flame until the tobacco glowed evenly.

He went on. "Sivad is trying to make points for his organization. That's about it. I can't see how you can get hurt."

"What about Israel?" asked David. "Can it get hurt?"

"Only its pride, David."

"No stigma on the American people when we didn't raise our voices against him?"

"Not really. The proverbial tempest in a teapot." Harry frowned. "I still don't like it."

"What's to like?" said Jonathan wryly. "Unless you're queer for poison." Then, seriously: "Has to be something more than just points, Lippy."

"I agree with Lippy," said Al. "No trouble for you, David. In a couple of weeks Sivad'll be back in his hole making bombs that'll explode in his face."

David turned to Myrna. "You're very quiet."

"I was thinking we ought to liquidate Yassim Sivad." She said it simply. Without rancor. "Sivad is a treacherous animal. Of course, he means trouble. Not only for you David, but for the world. Like a plague. He'll kill us if we don't get to him first."

Silence.

David broke it with: "You don't mean it, Myrna."

She sighed. "No, I don't mean it. Only because liquidation is against our principles. But it's a good idea," she added.

Lipman put down his pipe. "I have some news that's more disturbing than Sivad's visit." He paused. Then: "I got a call from our agent in Berlin."

David's eyebrows went up.

"Klaus Wagner just flew in from Libya," said Lipman. "With ten million dollars' worth of Arab money. Now *that* could mean trouble."

David nodded. "That could do his Nazi movement a lot of good."

"You could be the prime target, David," said Harry. "You've blocked him at every turn. And now that the Nazis are making headway . . ."

Myrna said, "With that kind of money he could hire an army to set you up."

"Klaus Wagner is a subtle thinker," said Jonathan. "Assassination is not his usual M.O."

Myrna's almond eyes went to slits. "He's a neo-Nazi, Jonathan. Not a very subtle cult."

"Jonathan," said David. "Did you know that Klaus Wagner's father once blew up three synagogues and two churches in Rome? During a Yom Kippur service and a high mass? Like father, like son, maybe?"

"I withdraw the observation," grinned Jonathan.

David returned the grin, then looked at Harry.

"What does it take," said Harry, "to transform an ultraconservative into a Nazi? Power? You can buy a lot of it for ten million dollars. I think it's only a down payment. There's more where it came from. I think we should stay on his tail. And at the same time keep an eye on Sivad."

"Al?"

"Instead of theorizing, David, why don't we wait for a move, then counter."

"We've never operated that way, Al."

"Come on, Al," said Harry. "What if we're faced with a fait accompli? Let's find out why he came and stop him."

David thought a moment, then: "What do you think, Lippy?"

Lipman tapped his pipe against a tray to empty the ashes. "Harry's right," he said. "Berlin wouldn't call unless they suspected something big in the works." He blew on the pipe stem to remove the burnt particles that clung to the sides of the bowl. "We'd better find out what brought him here."

"Okay." David turned to the group. "There goes your weekend shot to hell. We'll forget Sivad for the time being and work on Wagner." He checked his watch. "It's almost sundown. If there's anything else, let's hear it."

"I heard from Vegas," said Lipman. "Caesar's Palace wants to sponsor a baccarat showdown between you and an Arab sheikh. Continuous action. Each stake five million. One of the networks will clear time and pay a million to the winner."

"Sounds good," said David. "When?"

"Two weeks from today. Beginning at eight in the evening."

David frowned. "You know I don't work on the Sabbath."

"That's the way the sheikh wants it."

"Then forget it."

"You can take him, David. The hospital can use the funds."

"I said forget it." His voice was soft but his jaw tightened.

Lipman began filling his pipe. "Sure," he said.

David rose. "We'll meet Sunday morning."

He left for synagogue.

# 4

## New York City
## Saturday

It was warm for April. Warm and smoggy. The sun combined with the floating filth of the air to form an atmospheric sewage. The air offered you a whiff of its poison and you had no choice but to accept it.

*It did not affect the flight of the pigeons nearing the U.N. Plaza.*

David stood on the altar of the Thirty-eighth Street Synagogue holding the scroll of the Torah aloft, and in the traditional manner made a full turn before seating himself.

A member of the congregation tied the scrolls together with a ribbon, then covered it with a blue velvet casing bearing an image of the Tablet in golden, glittering threads.

David rested the Torah across his shoulder, closed his eyes and tried to listen to the reading of the haftarah. But the singsong rendition in Hebrew lulled his senses. He drifted into a semi-wakefulness that stirred memories of how he had come to build a synagogue in the heart of the garment district where no one resided but the rabbi.

*In the winter, when the days were short, the workers would pray the evening service before the subways carried them home to Brooklyn or the Bronx or Queens. And in the morning, they would come to don their tefillin before going off to their day's labors.*

*The synagogue was plain, no fancy trappings. It was a replica of the one his grandfather built in a small town in Germany.*

*Later burned to the ground by the Hitler youth.*

*But his father had described it exactly the way it had been. And that was the way David had built it. Exactly. From his father's description; from his own hazy memory of it when he was two years old. As he watched them put the torch to it.*

*The memory was vivid. The return home. His mother in a bloodbath. Raped. Slashed. Mutilated.*

*His father mad with anguish.*

*Their escape to Holland with the aid of a Catholic priest. Father Vogel. It cost the priest his life. So young.*

*In South Dakota, high on a mountaintop a plain, Catholic church was built in his honor. Father Vogel had often talked about wanting to settle in America; in South Dakota.*

*Alongside the church was the Father Vogel Sum-*

mer Camp for Boys. Funds provided from an unknown source. In perpetuity.

But the people of South Dakota somehow knew where the funds came from.

Thoughts of Klaus Wagner intruded.

Twenty years ago. It was on David's eighteenth birthday that he first met Wagner. In London.

David, the wunderkind, called in as a consultant to stabilize Britain's failing economy.

Klaus Wagner, only a couple of years older than David, preparing his hoodlums to desecrate London's synagogues and temples.

The plan aborted; a stoolie provided the information to Scotland Yard.

Wagner untouched. At a table in a pub with some toughs he boasted that next time he wouldn't fail.

David moved from the bar to Wagner's table, identified himself as a Jew and tossed a full glass of ale in the smirking Aryan face of the Nazi.

They beat him unmercifully.

The factor that started David's study of the art of using his hands as weapons.

Several years later in Paris he exposed members of the neo-Nazi party in high places in government led by Klaus Wagner.

In Monte Carlo he beat Wagner out of a million dollars of syndicate money, forcing Wagner to flee the syndicate's wrath.

Klaus went underground for five years. During that time David's life led him into other activities where retribution was called for. Klaus Wagner's voice was stilled.

Then the neo-Nazi movement began to make an appearance in America. It hardly caused a ripple. At first. But it began to grow and David began to take *heed. But no sign of Klaus Wagner until now. In New York.* With Arab backing.

The rabbi gently touched David's shoulder. "David?"

David came back to reality with a start.

"The Torah should be returned to the ark," said the rabbi.

"Sorry, rabbi." He got up and placed the Law in the ark murmuring the accompanying prayer.

He returned to his seat on the altar to finish the service.

The Lexington Avenue express left Grand Central on schedule. At Eighty-sixth Street Harry was to meet Pablo. On the forward end of the platform.

Pablo always had bits and pieces of information to sell. Harry was his best customer. They'd meet once a week on the station platform to complete the transaction. Sometimes Pablo had good stuff; most times it was inconsequential. But he was a good contact. *Houseboy for the deputy director of the FBI.*

This time he had something big. A tape, he'd told Harry over the phone: Worth five C's. A bargain. Names.

Harry wanted to know what names.

Pablo wouldn't tell him. Cash transaction.

No deal.

Pablo relented. One name was Klaus Wagner.

Harry sat in the front car of the train. He was not thinking of Pablo or the tape or Klaus Wagner.

*Yassim Sivad.*

The terrorist who, in six days, would stand at the lectern in the General Assembly and exhort the nations of the world to move toward the extermination of Israel.

Not Harry's worry. The threat against David Ring was what worried Harry.

A tie-in? Sivad-Wagner? PLO-Nazi? David Ring in the middle?

Worries lingered without logic.

The train stopped at Fifty-ninth Street, then was once again rocking and roaring along the ancient roadbed.

Pablo, a slightly-built, dark-haired man, hurried through the turnstile of the Eighty-sixth Street station and made his way to the forward end of the platform.

A tall black man was close behind.

Pablo glanced at his watch, then leaned over the edge and looked along the track.

He did not notice the black man.

The people on the platform were impressed with the black man's height. He had to be close to seven feet tall.

Pablo straightened up; he'd heard the train approaching. He savored the thought of five crisp hundred dollar bills.

Harry got out of his seat as the train began to slow for the Eighty-sixth Street stop. He moved to the center door. Others came up behind him.

The train roared in, slowed. It was a car-length away from the stop when the wheels screamed as the brakes suddenly went on, sending passengers catapulting.

Harry grabbed at a stanchion. He saw the motorman bolt from the cab, and out the front door.

The motorman leaped to the roadbed, Harry directly behind him. They knelt beside the still form of Pablo.

"I'm a doctor," said Harry, skimming his hands over Pablo's body, searching for the reel of tape.

"He didn't fall!" The motorman's eyes, filled with horror, stared at Harry. "Somebody pushed him! I couldn't stop in time!"

"It wouldn't have mattered," said Harry.

The knife was buried deep in Pablo's side.

There was no tape.

Harry climbed onto the platform and was instantly surrounded by people anxious to help. They'd seen it happen. They described the black man as if they had the picture in front of them. They'd already called the police.

David Ring's network of agents moved faster than New York's finest.

They had more talent.

Stronger connections.

A better raison d'être.

In less than an hour Harry knew where the black man could be found.

He made a deal with Detective Lieutenant Brady.

## New York City, East Village
## Saturday

They say that some parts of the East Village are not so bad. But all agree that most parts are crummy.

In the early 1960's the flower children liked the crummy parts so much they settled there. And became weeds. They could be seen wilting in the doorways. It seemed so long ago.

Harry and Brady, a tall man with wide shoulders, stepped over a drug-filled but still breathing form blocking the doorway of a tenement building. They entered a dark hallway and started their climb to the sixth floor.

The crumbling structure had been condemned for two years, yet the tenants still paid rent.

The sixth floor had a pair of doors facing the front and a pair at the rear.

The information was that the black man lived in the back, on the right side. The flat on the left was vacant.

Harry knocked.

No answer.

He knocked again and placed his ear to the door. There was a rustling sound inside. Then silence.

Harry signaled Brady to conceal himself in the doorway of the vacant apartment. Harry then made a noisy descent of the stairs and tiptoed quietly back up. He joined Brady.

A bolt on the door of the occupied flat slid open and the tall black man stepped out into the hallway to peer down the stairwell.

"Looking for someone?" said Harry.

The black man whirled. When he realized what had happened he smiled. It was the smile of a man whose mind was not smiling.

"You did that pretty," he said. Then he saw Brady's badge. And his gun. He stopped smiling.

They backed the big man into the flat, through a narrow hall and into a windowless, smoke-filled room.

Brady frisked the man and Harry said, "Give me the tape."

"What tape?"

Brady pointed his gun at the man and pulled back the hammer.

"Cops ain't supposed to do that," the black man said.

Harry took the gun from Brady and pointed it at the prisoner. "I'm just an apprentice civilian," said

Harry grinning. "If I killed you the cop will swear it was self-defense."

"Right," said Brady.

Harry reached up and touched the barrel of the .38 to the tall black man's temple. "Once more. Hand over the tape."

The man's eyes rolled. "You win, man." He strode to a cupboard.

Harry handed the gun back to Brady.

The black man opened a drawer, rummaged through it and came up with a small reel.

*In his left hand.*

*His right held an automatic.*

Brady shot him before he could use it.

"Too bad," said Harry, looking down on the sprawled corpse. "I wanted to find out who he was working for."

"Can't win 'em all," said Brady.


## New York City, Harlem
## Saturday

Jonathan walked into the Blue Grotto Bar and Grill and sat in a booth that had a sign over it in huge letters: KING.

King Modecai, a Jamaican, a gambler, a winner.

No one but King was allowed to sit in King's booth. Except by special invitation. Jonathan had been invited.

A waitress came over and Jonathan ordered a bourbon and water.

The bar was packed with drinkers. The tables were filled. The steady hum of conversation filled the air.

The girl brought the drink. On the house. When

you sat in King's booth you were a guest of the establishment.

Jonathan abstractedly twirled the ice in the glass with his finger. If he had his way, he'd dispose of both Sivad and Wagner. But it wasn't David's way. Of course David was right. That's why he was David. He remembered when David took him, his mother and his four sisters out of the black ghetto and made them feel like they belonged to the human race; gave them education and self-respect and a work ethic. In return Jonathan offered him his life. David asked only for his wits.

The conversation around him halted abruptly. The room went silent.

King had walked in.

It was only after King took his seat in his booth that the place returned to normal.

"How do you feel, Johnnie?" began King.

"Great. And you?"

"Nevuh bettah." His voice was soft and mellow, rich like the lower register of a cultured baritone.

He was a huge man, black as anthracite. But his hair was as white as the teeth he showed when he smiled.

He wore a long white coat buttoned at the throat, white duck pants and matching buckskin shoes.

He had long arms and enormous hands.

And one kidney. He'd taken a bullet in the other one; a bullet that was meant for David Ring.

When the one kidney failed, David rounded up donors from all over the world.

King's body rejected them all.

He had lived on a machine.

Until David presented him with one of his own kidneys.

It held.

Complete affinity.

It happened long ago.

King spoke again. "I don't know how or what they gonna do, Johnnie. But they got the blueprints. All I can relate to you is that Davey is in the center of the cross hairs. That don't mean a hit, Johnnie. All it mean is bye-bye, baby. . . . Davey have got a big organization so he can take care. If he need me, he got me. . . . If I get more info, I pass it on. At this precise point in time I got nothin' but worry. So you tell Davey to keep jabbin' with his left and have his right ready to do the damage."

He caught his breath. "That Wagner . . . he tricky."

Jonathan rose. "Thanks, King." He handed him an envelope.

King passed it back. "Don't insult me, Johnnie."

"My apologies." Jonathan bowed himself out.

"Shalom," murmured King.


## New York City, Yorkville
## Saturday

There weren't many customers in the coffeehouse on East Eighty-sixth Street when Al walked in. Those who were there were dawdling over their coffee reading the *Staats-Zeitung* or *Der Spiegel*.

Al went past the man behind the register, nodded a greeting, then disappeared through a curtained doorway in the rear to enter a small storeroom. A thick steel door led to the cellar. Al had a key that opened it.

At the bottom of the stairs he opened another door with a twist of the knob.

A wave of conversation and mingled laughter greeted him as he walked in.

It did not look much like a cellar. The walls were of knotty pine; the floor carpeted. Along the back was a well-stocked bar.

Al managed to reach the bar without too much jostling. "Scotch and soda, please."

The bartender nodded.

Al looked up at the picture that hung on the back wall. It was a photo of a large, handsome man with blond hair cropped in military style.

Klaus Wagner.

"This is the biggest crowd we've had yet," said the bartender. He handed Al the drink, then leaned in close. "Hoffman's here, you know."

"I know," said Al.

The bartender jerked his head at the crowd. "Look at that mob. They came from all over the country."

A thin, ascetic man with a yellowish tinge to his skin handed an empty glass to the bartender. "*Wieder einmal, bitte.*"

"*Spritzer?*" asked the bartender.

"*Ja.*"

The man held out his hand to Al. "Hans Grenzig. Chicago Police Commission."

Al shook his hand. "Alfred Michaels. David Ring infiltrator."

"*Wunderbar!*" The man laughed appreciatively at what he took to be a joke.

The bartender handed him the drink.

"*Danke.*" He turned to Al. "*Auf Wiedersehen.*" Then he winked. "Soon, my friend. Very soon."

"When do you think?"

The man smiled and moved into the crowd.

"That guy is really a big shot," said the bartender.

"Yeah," said Al. "Chicago police. Can't be much bigger than that."

"Except in Washington, huh?" The bartender leered.

Al winked at him. "Who in Washington, do you suppose?"

"I wouldn't want to know," said the bartender flatly. He moved away to rinse glasses.

Snatches of conversation as Al mingled:

*It must have been quite a meeting last night.*

*Where was it?*

*Hoffman will tell us about it.*

*I know Klaus Wagner's in town.*

*My group is ready.*

*L.A. and Frisco are working together.*

Dwight Hoffman entered from a side door dressed in full military uniform complete with swastikas. He was a man of medium height, almost totally bald, but he held himself stiffly erect.

He waited for the sounds in the room to subside. Then in sharp, staccato tones:

"I have spoken with Klaus Wagner. . . . Immediately after the meeting at Lake George. . . . He has directed me . . . to notify you . . . to prepare . . . for Alert Z."

He paused, his jaw jutting, his face rigid.

Audience silent. Expectant.

He continued. "You will receive the signal . . . within a short time. . . . You are to leave here at once . . . to advise your units . . . accordingly. . . . We are on the verge . . . of a tremendous victory. . . . Go! God is with us!"

He gave the Nazi salute.

*Sieg Heil! Sieg Heil! Sieg Heil!*

They started to move out. Al with them.

"Alfred Michaels!"

Al turned to see Hoffman beckoning.

"Please."

Hoffman stood stiffly waiting for Al to reach him.

What a stuffed pig, thought Al. He'd have liked to break his face open. Right there. As he once did to a loudmouthed Jew-hater in a bar. That was before he joined David's organization.

Al was a former CIA undercover agent. Resigned because of his superior's veiled antisemitism. And Al, a non-Jew.

"Alfred," began Hoffman, "Klaus Wagner wishes me . . . to convey his greetings . . . and to compliment you on your fine . . . work."

"Thank him for me, Herr Hoffman."

Hoffman offered him a crooked smile. "Soon . . . you will be able to do that . . . in person." He beckoned. "Come . . . I have a surprise for you."

They walked down a short corridor to another room. Klaus Wagner stood up as they entered. He was pointing a .357 Magnum at Al.

Hoffman smirked.

Al cursed himself for his carelessness. He should have been forewarned by Hoffman's oiliness; his condescending manner, the look of anticipation.

"We are in a war, Alfred," said Wagner softly. "A double agent in a war is a dangerous profession."

"What?" Al took a step forward. *Time. Play for time.*

"Don't move!"

"You're mistaken, Herr Wagner." *Keep him talking.*

"I cannot afford the luxury of debating it," said Wagner.

Al talked fast. "I've got certain information you

could make use of and at the same time put David Ring on ice." He reached into his inside pocket. "I've got something here—"

Al tried to duck as he pulled out his own gun. Too late.

Wagner's Magnum blew his face open.

## New York City, Harlem
## Saturday

The steel skeleton of a building reached twenty stories high. Surrounding it a square block of tenements had been leveled.

A sign read:

SITE OF THE DAVID RING CHILDREN'S
HOSPITAL AND PLAYGROUND

The watchman, an elderly black man, came out of a trailer office to join David Ring. They stood viewing the structure for a moment. "It's gettin' there," said the watchman.

David nodded.

"You know what my dumb old lady say? She say, 'That Mister Ring—his skin may be white, but underneath his heart is as black as ours.' Ain't that a dumb thing?"

David laughed. "But we know what she meant, don't we, Henry?"

"But that's dumb." Henry reentered the office shaking his head.

David wandered within the skeletal structure, paused, looked around; memories flooding. Thirty years ago it was a rubble-strewn lot where they had played touch football.

"Hey, Jonathan—gotta be quick. . . . Watch it, Harry . . . Myrna—Al—you'll never touch me. . . . Come on, Lippy . . . Hafez—move—move—"

Hafez, the little Arab boy who played with them; and was picked up every day by the chauffeur-driven sedan.

"Wheeee! Touch me if you can, Lippy!"

He remembered when he tripped and fell and the ball flew out of his hands. Lippy had scooped it up and was about to start for the goal when he noticed that David lay still. He stopped. Concerned.

Myrna cried: "He's hurt!"

Lipman dropped the ball, bent over him; turned him on his back. At that instant, David leaped to his feet, grabbed the ball and gleefully raced to the goal line.

Lipman was furious. "That wasn't fair!"

David returned slowly. "You're right, Lippy," he said. "It was a dirty trick. But you should always be on guard."

"Even against your friends?" said Lipman bitterly.

David's face grew sober. "Especially against friends, Lippy. It's easy to be on guard against your enemies."

The automobile horn sounded; the chauffeur coming to pick up Hafez.

Hafez, his face filled with pain, turned to David. "I must go, David," he said, trembling. "I won't be able to play with you again." He lowered his eyes. "My father . . . has forbidden me . . . to play with a Jew."

He looked up at David. "I love you, David," he said in a whisper. "Salaam."

Tears filled his eyes as he hurried away to the limousine.

"Shalom, Hafez," said David under his breath.

41

The group watched silently as Hafez got into the car.

Its license plate read: UN DELEGATE.

It was then David vowed to himself he'd be the most powerful Jew in the world.

# 5

## New York City
## Sunday

*The pigeons left their cote from atop a building on lower Broadway and headed northeast.*

The group was assembled in the conference room in the David Ring Building.

David came in with a worried look. "Anyone hear from Al?"

"Not since last night," said Jonathan. "He told me he was going to attend a meeting at the Yorkville Coffee House."

"He got word that Dwight Hoffman was in town," said Harry.

David shook his head, troubled. "It's not like Al not to check in. . . . Go ahead, Harry. Let's hear the tape."

"It came off a tap on Carl Fredericks' phone on Thursday. It cost Pablo his life." Harry pressed the start button, and they heard seven tones from the push-button phone. Then:

FREDERICKS: *Hello, Bob. Carl.*

BOB: *Yes, Carl?*

FREDERICKS: *I'm picking up Klaus Wagner at the airport tomorrow. Notify the others. We'll meet tomorrow evening.*

BOB: *The usual place?*

FREDERICKS: *Right. Eight o'clock. Plan to spend the night.*

BOB: *I know Marley can make it. But I'm not sure that Brandon or Franklyn can get out of Washington in time.*

FREDERICKS: *Just tell them that Klaus has the makings. They'll be there.*

BOB: *I'll get right on it.*

FREDERICKS: *Good. See you tomorrow.*

Harry turned off the machine. "We were unable to locate the meeting place. I was hoping Al could tell us."

"You had the phone tones analyzed?" said David.

Harry nodded. "Unlisted number for Reverend Robert Carson."

"What have you got, Myrna?" David noticed she held the computer printout.

"Just a record of Wagner's little helpers."

She read: "Reverend Robert Carson . . . Fascist par excellence. Spiritual director of the United Freedom Church of America. Received a commendation from Senator Franklyn, quote—'for your unselfish devotion to God and Country.'" She looked up. "Want to hear about the senator?"

David smiled. "I know more about him than the computer." He recited: ". . . censured by the Senate body for demaguery, lame duck, sole owner of Lynfrank Electronics. . . . There's more but it loses in translation. Now, what about Marley?"

Myrna continued with the printout. "General Marley, U.S. Army, Retired. Super hawk, super political. Relieved of command by President Eisenhower. Chairman of the Board of Techno Chemical Corporation."

"Know anything about that outfit, Lippy?" asked David.

Lipman removed the pipe from between his teeth before he replied. "Big government contracts. Explosives, mainly. They're the ones who hold the patent on Perplax."

David nodded. "Percussive plastique."

"Banned by Congress for export," said Lipman. "A devilish little item."

"Second cousin to the atomic warhead," said David. He pointed to Myrna's sheet. "What's it say about Fredericks?"

"Carl Fredericks—found guilty of gross negligence in killing of unarmed suspect. Pardoned by President Wentworth and permitted to retain his post as deputy director of FBI." She put the paper down. "The rest is ancient background. No gems. Nothing special on Secretary of State Brandon."

"Thanks, Myrna . . . Did you come up with anything, Jonathan?"

"You're being set up for something. What, how, when—I drew a blank. But King said definitely no hit."

"Lippy, is there any way I can be ruined financially?"

"No way."

"Conspiracy?" asked David. "Lay me open to a charge of treason . . . or murder, maybe?" He closed his eyes. "Or—'*Jewish philanthropist exposed as in-*

*ternational dealer in drugs!*' " He tossed Lipman an enigmatic look. "That would be a sensational frame. But they couldn't get away with it, could they? Unless it's something bigger . . ."

Silence.

Myrna moved the printout across to David. "There's the makings for your setup," she said softly. "You can't kill a snake by stepping on its tail. The head, David. One slice at the head."

Harry stood up. "David . . ."

David held up his hand. "I know. Your Yassim Sivad hunch. . . . Myrna, run a calendar check for the rest of the month. See if you can nail down a happening other than Sivad's visit. One that Wagner can make use of. Meanwhile, let's figure that Sivad is Wagner's tie-in.

"Jonathan, you and Harry cover General Marley. We *must* know where that meeting took place. Myrna, call our friends in Washington and see what they can come up with."

He rose; the group with him. "I'll go to Yorkville and try to find out what happened to Al. . . . Lippy, stay by the phone."

"Take care," said Lippy.

As they filed out, Lipman began to load his pipe.

# 6

## Smithtown, Long Island
## Sunday

The main building of the Techno Chemical Corporation was set back from the highway behind acres of lush, closely cropped lawn. Three stories high, the granite walls covered with English ivy. The driveway leading to it, paved in black asphalt, was bordered with boxwood.

Were it not for the sign over the front gate reading TECHNO CHEMICAL CORPORATION, the property might have been mistaken for that of a small college, or convent, or an exclusive sanitarium. But hardly the home of Perplax, one of the deadliest products the mind of man had yet conceived.

A small van drove up to the front gate. The driver handed a card to the guard.

The guard eyed the driver curiously. A *delivery on Sunday? If not a delivery, why the van? A pickup?*

The guard shrugged and went into his booth. He placed the card in the machine, pressed the necessary buttons; the light flashed green. He returned the card to the driver, nodding him on.

The van proceeded along the asphalt, around the rear of the building to a loading platform. Three large cartons were waiting to be picked up.

The driver loaded them into the van.

## Long Island City, New York
## Sunday

Across the top of the factory building, letters were strung out to spell: LYNFRANK ELECTRONICS.

The van made another pickup.

## Jersey City, New Jersey
## Sunday

The van, its rear doors open, was parked in an alley at the back door of a warehouse. The driver sat smoking; waiting.

The door opened and a man emerged with an armful of police uniforms. The driver snuffed out his cigarette as the man placed the uniforms in the van.

"What kind did you get?" asked the driver, leaning out of the window.

"Assorted Special Service mainly—that's what they asked for." He closed the doors of the van and went around to the driver.

"As soon as you leave," he said, "I'll reconnect the burglar alarm, then set it off."

"Right. You're a good soldier."

The good soldier gave the Nazi salute.

The driver started the engine and headed the van toward Lake George.

# 7

## New York City—Yorkville
## Sunday

The coffeehouse on Eighty-sixth Street was bustling.
The man behind the cash register was so busy he
hadn't noticed David waiting. Not until he had finished with the last customer in a long line.

The man at the register was big. Heavy. Florid.
Patches under his eyes filled with fluid. Kidney prob-
lem, perhaps. Or an elevated blood pressure. No
doubt he didn't look well normally. But his pallor
turned noticeably worse when David stood before
him.

"Yes, Mr. Ring?" he said guardedly.

"Where can I find Hoffman?"

"I don't know. Is he in town?"

"Yes," said David quietly. "He's in town."

"Is that so! And he never stopped in to say hello. Tsk, tsk. Imagine that."

A customer arrived with his check.

"Excuse me, Mr. Ring," said the man. He rang up the change. As the transaction was proceeding, David headed toward the curtain at the back.

The man signaled a waiter to take his place at the register, then hurried after his unwelcome guest.

David was examining the steel door in the back room when the man came in, breathing heavily.

"What are you doing here, Mr. Ring?" he demanded.

"Open this," said David.

"You have no right to—"

"Open it," interrupted David.

The man paused, his swollen eyes filled with a smoldering hate. "Let me tell you something, Mr. Ring," he began. "You are a very important man. The whole world knows who you are. You are worth millions. Yet you go around the city like a common person. Well, to me that's exactly what you are—a common person." He spat the rest of it. "So get the hell out of my place or I'll call the police." *That's the way to talk to the* Schweinhund *millionaire Jew!* the man thought. *Soon! Klaus Wagner would take care of them all!*

Luxuriating in his thoughts the man paid little attention as David placed a heavy wooden milk crate on its side, until . . .

David emitted an unholy, primal scream. The edge of his hand flashed downward in a blur of speed. The crate was sliced cleanly in two.

"Unlock the door," said David calmly, "or I'll do that to your face."

The big man's florid face turned ashen. He unlocked

the door. Together they went down the stairs into the meeting room, into the anteroom where Al's blood was a dark stain on the floor.

David knew.

He closed his eyes; tears escaped as he recited the Kaddish aloud.

Al Michaels was Catholic. David would arrange a requiem mass.

"Who was at the meeting yesterday?" asked David.

The man was trembling. "Hoffman and Klaus Wagner."

"Where are they?"

"I don't know. I swear it! I wasn't at the meeting. I was upstairs and left before the meeting finished. Please believe me." He clasped his hands as if in prayer.

David stared at the stain on the floor. He knew what had to be done. There'd never be another Bund meeting here. Never.

David went in search of a certain street singer. A little old German who accompanied himself on the accordion. Comic songs were his specialty. Also information. He rarely disappointed David in either.

> *"Wenn meine Frau mich ärgern tut*
> *So weiss ich was ich tu."*

There he was, his hat on the sidewalk at his feet; the Sunday people gathered around.

He spotted David. They exchanged looks.

> *"Steck' ich sie in einen Hafersack*
> *Und bind' ihn oben zu."*

The people laughed.

> *"So dann wird sie bitten*
> *Lieber Mann mach doch auf*

*Nehm ich einen Hammerstiel*
*Und* have *noch darauf."*

The people liked the song. They laughed and dropped coins in the hat then drifted away.

The singer stooped to empty the hat as a fifty dollar bill fluttered into it. He smiled up at David. *"Danke,"* he said, straightening up.

*"Bitte,"* replied David. "I enjoyed your song very much."

"You would like to hear something else?"

"Yes."

"I would be pleased."

"I'm looking for Dwight Hoffman."

"He is in town?"

"Yes."

"You are in a hurry?"

"Yes."

"Give me one hour."

"I have thirty minutes." He handed him another fifty.

"I will try."

"Good."

"You know my room?"

David nodded. "A half hour."

The little German singer hurried away.

David called Lipman to arrange for the destruction of the coffeehouse. Only symbolic. It wouldn't bring Al back.

He called the monsignor at St. Patrick's Cathedral and arranged for a mass for Al.

A half hour later he entered the dingy hallway of the rooming house where the little German singer lived.

The stairs were wooden; the sounds of David's footsteps echoed as he climbed.

He walked along the third-floor corridor until he came to the singer's room. The door was slightly ajar.

David knocked, then pushed the door open wide. "Erich?" He walked in slowly.

It was a small room with a couple of chairs and well-worn sofa that apparently opened into a bed. A divider separated the room from a tiny kitchen.

"Erich?" He checked his watch, then noticed the bathroom door was closed. David moved to it, knocked, and again called, "Erich?"

No answer.

He turned the knob; opened the door slightly.

The bathtub had overflowed; the little German singer was submerged, fully clothed, his sightless eyes bulging.

"Damn them!" David cried. He lifted the little man out of the tub and gently laid him on the sofa. "Sorry, Erich," he murmured as he closed the staring eyes. "Death follows me like a shadow. I should have found another way and left you to your *Lieder*."

He noticed the accordion on the table, lonely as if mourning its master's touch. He placed it alongside the singer's body. The bellows expanded and gave forth a weeping wail. There was also a matchbook cover.

In pencil it told David: 15 West 91.

Hoffman was in the apartment on West Ninety-first Street. So were Klaus Wagner and Anna Thornton.

"It will not be easy, Anna," Wagner was telling her. "But if anyone can do it, you can."

"Sure," she said dubiously. "But how close can a woman get to a man who has no history of romantic involvement."

"You'll manage."

"Why would he start now?"

"Because you are special. With special talents," grinned Wagner, his frigid blue eyes appraising her obvious charms.

Hoffman leered, his bald head gleaming. "Special enough . . . to have become . . . the mistress of the president of the United States."

She gave him a cold stare then swung her look to Wagner.

"I'll do the best I can." She placed a minicamera in her handbag together with a full hypodermic syringe swathed in cotton. The intercom sounded. Wagner and Hoffman exchanged puzzled looks. Wagner nodded for Hoffman to answer the buzzer.

Hoffman pressed the button and said: "Yes?"

David stood in front of the locked iron-grilled door of the narrow three-story residence. He had just pressed the button alongside the name: *Carl Fredericks, apartment* 2G.

"I have a package for Mr. Hoffman," said David into the intercom."

"Who is the package from?"

"Klaus Wagner."

The room froze. Then Wagner smiled. "We are very lucky, Anna. That happens to be David Ring." He motioned for her to get into the bathroom.

David waited. And after a while the door lock was released and he entered. He crossed the lobby, taking the stairs instead of the elevator.

He paused at the door marked 2G. Listening. No sound.

He pressed the button. A bell chimed.

"Come in," Hoffman's voice from inside. "The door is not locked."

David opened the door and looked into the muzzle

of a Luger. Above it was Hoffman's malevolent face. David stood there, impassive.

*"Come in. Come in, Mr. Ring."* From Klaus Wagner. Hoffman stepped aside for David to enter. The door closed behind him.

He gazed into the cold eyes of Klaus Wagner. The memory of their other encounters flooded. He should have killed him when he had the chance. But there would have been others to take his place. There had to be another way.

"So you have a package for Mr. Hoffman?" smirked Klaus Wagner. "From me, yet, eh?"

The humor wasn't lost on David. "I guess I should have chosen another name," he said dryly.

"What do you want, Mr. Ring?"

He turned to Hoffman. "Put the gun away. You're not going to use it."

"I'll ask you again," said Wagner. "What do you want?"

"If Mr. Hoffman doesn't get rid of that gun I'll break his arm."

Hoffman's face darkened. The Luger was leveled point blank.

*"Nein!"* shouted Klaus.

David sprang. He got Hoffman's arm in a crushing hold. The gun clattered to the floor. At the same instant he pressed a finger to Hoffman's neck.

Hoffman folded; unconscious.

"You're still playing strong man, Mr. Ring," said Wagner.

"And you, Herr Wagner?" said David. "What are you playing? Your usual murderous games? What do you intend to do with ten million dollars of Arab blood money? Buy off a few politicians? *For every million dollars you spend I have a hundred times that much to counter it!"*

"You are losing your cool, Mr. Ring," said Wagner softly.

Hoffman regained consciousness, one arm hanging limp. David did not see him crawl painfully along the floor toward the gun.

He had it now—aimed at David's back.

David did not flinch when Wagner whipped his gun out and fired. Hoffman's body sprawled crazily, a bullet hole in his forehead.

"He was going to kill you, Mr. Ring," said Klaus. "I wouldn't want that to happen."

"Why?"

"I have other plans for you."

"Such as?"

"In due time." Wagner offered him a broad grin.

David started for the phone. "Meanwhile," he said, "we should call the police."

Wagner still held the gun. "That might embarrass me."

"I expect it would."

"Also it could affect my schedule of events negatively."

"Should I be concerned about that?" David dialed for the operator.

"Yes," nodded Wagner. "You should be concerned about that."

"Operator," said David into the phone, "get me the police." He tossed Wagner a curious look. "How do you mean?"

Wagner raised the gun. "I would no longer have a reason to keep you alive."

David paused, then slowly dropped the phone to its cradle. "So we're playing games, are we?"

"For big stakes, Mr. Ring."

"You're not in my league, Wagner."

"Perhaps not. But I have the advantage of time. And for you, time is running out."

David laughed. "I'll beat you and your kind, Wagner," he said. "Whatever your game is. Whatever your advantage."

He started for the door; then paused. Without turning, he said, "Who killed Al Michaels, you or Hoffman?"

Wagner shrugged. "I was forced to do it."

David stood for a moment looking grim; his face working. Then slowly he crossed back to him. "You're giving me points, Wagner," he said, barely above a whisper.

Wagner leveled his gun. "Stay where you are!"

"And if I don't, will you kill me?" He gave Wagner a cold smile. "That isn't your plan, Wagner. You have a reason to keep me alive, you said. But don't worry, I'm not going to harm you. It'd be relatively simple to dispose of you; but then I'd never learn what your plan is, would I? Could it go on without you Wagner? Would all action grind to a halt? If I was sure, I'd . . ."

With a lightning move, he snatched the gun from Wagner's hand. "Talk," he said softly, leveling the pistol, "or I'll blow your head off."

Wagner smiled. "You're not a murderer, Mr. Ring."

"Don't count on it."

"You're a religious man. Thou shalt not kill. Remember?"

"An eye for an eye, Wagner. Remember?"

"The commandments take precedence," said Wagner, sure of his ground.

David removed the bullets from the gun and handed it back to him. "Now sit down and we'll talk. But don't move or I'll shred your face."

He circled the chair in which Wagner sat. Wagner followed him with his eyes.

"Remember how your friends in the Third Reich had Stars of David stitched onto the Jews' clothing?" said David.

*Round and round he went.*

"Also the word '*Jude*'?"

*Circling . . . Circling . . .*

"And how about those numbers burned into their flesh in the concentration camps?"

Wagner's eyes kept following. *What was he up to?*

"Like branded calves . . ."

*Round and round . . .*

"Those were the days, weren't they, Wagner? The stench of burning flesh . . ."

*Round and round . . .*

". . . the screams and cries of tortured bodies . . ."

*Round and round . . .*

". . . the ovens, Wagner . . . the gas chambers . . ."

David pounced. The hand covered Wagner's mouth; the other held a small knife. He worked quickly. Smoothly. Deftly. Five seconds at the most.

David stepped back; and Wagner let out a horrible shriek.

Wagner's hands covered his forehead. Then he lowered them slowly, staring at the blood that stained them. "Jew pig!" he spat.

Blood dripped into his eyes.

*From the swastika engraved on his forehead!*

David started for the door. He paused, grinning. "Even Hitler knew that pigs and Jews had nothing in common. *Auf Wiedersehen*." He left, closing the door behind him.

Wagner, trembling, reached for the phone as Anna Thornton burst into the room from the bedroom. She stared at him, shocked.

"What happened?"

"Never mind!" said Wagner, harshly. "Intercept him before he reaches a phone. Stay with him as planned. Hurry!"

Anna moved out quickly.

"Carl!" Wagner's voice on the phone was thick. "Come to the apartment at once! I was forced to kill Hoffman . . ."

He was unable to continue. In the throes of hysteria he jumped to his feet. "I swear to God that I will finish what Hitler started!" he screamed, flailing his arms. "I will not fail! No! Never! Never!"

His mouth foaming, he fell to the floor; his body writhing in a grand mal epileptic seizure.

# 8

David made an anonymous phone call to the police from his car. But he was sure that by the time they got to the apartment, Fredericks would have the situation well in hand.

Just as he hung up the phone Anna came racing out of the building feigning panic. "Please—take me away from here . . ." She pulled the car door open and climbed in. "I was in the bedroom . . ." She began to sob. ". . . when he shot Hoffman . . . I ran out . . . after you left . . . please . . ."

David started the car. "Are you a friend of Hoffman's?" he asked, looking straight ahead.

"He was a client." She dabbed at her eyes with a handkerchief.

"A client?"

She nodded. "This Mr. Wagner wanted a girl . . .

Hoffman called me. I got there just before you did
. . . I saw it happen. He'll kill me!"

David gave her a sidelong glance. Damn attractive.
Should he play along? What could she be after?
Obviously part of the group. A good actress.

"I'm sure you know who I am," said David.

"Yes. David Ring. I heard it all. Most of it I didn't
understand."

"And who are you?"

"Anna Thornton. A very expensive hooker."

"I can afford you."

"It wasn't a pitch," she said coldly. "Just a description. At the moment I'm not selling."

He decided to take the bait. "I suggest," he said,
"that you stay in my apartment for a while. Until
Carl Fredericks settles Wagner's panic."

Anna's face registered total ingenuousness. "Oh, I
couldn't do that."

"Why not?" *She's playing it well*, he thought.

"I'd be taking advantage of . . ."

"I insist."

With just the right amount of hesitation, she said:
"Thank you."

General Marley and Klaus Wagner came out of the
Towers entrance of the Waldorf-Astoria and hurried
into a waiting cab. Wagner wore a felt hat, the brim
snapped down to cover the engraved swastika.

The cab started away; Harry and Jonathan not far
behind.

David stood behind the bar mixing a drink, his expression stolid but his mind smiling as he watched
Anna, seated on a barstool, performing on the phone.

"Hi, Twinkie baby," she cooed. "How is my little
Puzzino?" She paused to hear how her little Puzzino
was. Then she said, "I miss you, too." She made with

the kisses. "Feel better now?" She listened and winked at David. "I'm so glad . . . Twinkie, honey," she said sorrowfully, "I have to cancel our date, but I'll double your pleasure next time. Okay?"

Fredericks, on the phone from the apartment at 15 West Ninety-first Street, was playing the part of Puzzino. He was alone in the apartment.

"All okay now," said Fredericks. "I convinced the police it was FBI business. . . . Try to keep close to him until Friday. But be careful."

Anna continued with her act. "Of course Anna loves you. Good-bye, Twinkie. I'll call you." More kisses, followed by the disconnect.

She gave David an arch look. "That was a two-hundred-dollar trick I gave up for you, David."

David grinned. "All work and no play . . ."

"He's seventy-five years old and all I do for him is pelt his body with Ping-Pong balls. Not very hard work."

David began pouring his concoction. "The wags in Washington say that our bachelor president gets turned on that way."

"Oh?" Anna's guard went up.

He handed her the drink. It was in a two-ounce cocktail glass.

She sniffed it. "What do you call it?"

"Aphrodisia number two. Number one is for less hearty souls." He touched his glass to hers. "Works better than Ping-Pong balls."

He downed the drink while Anna tasted hers. "Mmmm . . . tastes better too, I bet."

"Finish it quickly," David said. "It's the second one that does the trick."

"If it works on me, I'll bottle it."

She drained the contents of the glass and David refilled it immediately. "Take your time with this one," he said in an academic tone. "From now on it becomes a matter of absorption."

Anna closed her eyes and whirled herself once around gently on the stool. "Mmmm—I feel good."

Another whirl.

Her eyes opened. "Have you got a steady girl? I know you're not married."

"How do you know?"

"Everybody knows about you. Millionaire bachelor. Philanthropist. Industrialist. Athlete. Gambler. Nemesis of the bad guys. Scholar. Fighter. Religious Jew . . ."

"You left out cuddly," he said with a straight face.

She laughed. "I have yet to find out about that."

"To answer your question, Anna," said David, moving close to her. "I don't have a steady girl." He kissed her gently. "How's the drink behaving?"

She took a few sips and thought it over.

"If you have to think about it, you're not ready," said David flatly.

She gave him a mischievous look. "I was ready the minute I walked in this room."

David studied her dark-eyed beauty closely for a moment. A consummate actress, he thought. Then he said: "Not the kind of ready I like."

"That's silly," she said sipping the drink. "I ought to know if I'm ready to make love to you."

"Say 'Sister Susie's sewing shirts for soldiers.' "

"What?"

"Say it."

"For Chrissake!"

"Say it."

"I will not. No!"

"Come on."

"No, no, N-o—No." She drained the glass and took

a once-around-whirl. "Sister Susie's sewing shits for . . ."

"You're nearly ready," he laughed.

"Jesus, David, what the hell kind of games do you play? What do I have to do to prove to you that I really want to—to—" Her eyes grew wide; her voice guttural. "Oh, my God!"

Her hands clenching and unclenching, her face aflame, she thrust her fingers in the collar of her dress and ripped it down the middle, exposing her breasts and her mini-bikini panties.

David lifted her in his arms. A beautiful bundle in fancy wrapping. There would be time tomorrow to find out what her game was. He'd find out. No question. Meanwhile . . .

She kissed him fiercely, moaning as he carried her into the bedroom.

The cab drove through the entrance to the airfield and stopped at the dispatcher's office. A Lear Jet Executive was parked nearby, its two jet engines warming.

Outside the chain link fence, Harry Riordon peered through his binoculars and saw the dispatcher in earnest conversation with Marley and Wagner.

Then they exchanged Nazi salutes and entered the plane.

Harry put down the glasses. "David will want to know where they're headed."

Jonathan agreed. "It may be a long wait before the pilot gets back."

"We can't afford the time," said Harry. "Let's try the dispatcher."

Jonathan started the motor and drove through the gate.

The dispatcher came out of the office to meet the

car. He was heavy, flabby. His pig eyes flickered with suspicion.

"Good-evening," said Jonathan.

The dispatcher nodded.

"I wonder if you could tell us the destination of the plane that just took off," said Harry politely.

"Are you a cop?"

"No."

"I don't give out that information." He turned to go back into his office.

"Hold it."

The dispatcher paused; turned his head.

Harry flashed a hundred-dollar bill. "Just for a short answer to my question."

"Tax free," added Jonathan.

The dispatcher curled a thick lip and said, "Shove it." He went into the office.

Harry and Jonathan exchanged looks, then got out of the car. When they walked into the office the dispatcher was behind a desk leveling a .45.

"If you ain't outa here in five seconds," he said, expressionless, "I'll call the cops." He reached for the phone.

They drove out of the field and parked a quarter of a mile away.

They returned on foot. Carefully.

There was no activity on the field. The single hangar housed two helicopters. Each bore the name TECHNO CHEMICAL CORP.

"This must be General Marley's private little field," whispered Jonathan.

Harry nodded. "And the dispatcher must be Marley's private little Nazi."

They closed in on the office. The door was open. The dispatcher was seated at the radio transmitter flush against the rear wall, his back to the door.

"I don't know who they were," he said into the mike. "But I thought I ought to tell you about it." He listened, his headset tight over his ears so that he only heard what was being transmitted. He did not hear Harry open the desk drawer and remove the .45.

Jonathan stood directly behind the man waiting for him to finish.

"Yes, sir," said the dispatcher. "I understand. I'll wait for the pilot to get back. Anything else?" Apparently not. "Have a good meeting. Over and out."

The dispatcher flipped several levers on the board to shut off communication, then stood up and removed his headset. He turned. His eyes bulged in shock at the sight of the hard-looking black man in front of him.

Jonathan jammed his forearm against the man's throat, forcing his head against the transmitter panel.

The man made a choking sound; his face grimaced in pain.

Jonathan punched him in the pit of the stomach. The air came with a *whoosh*.

"Tell us the plane's destination," said Jonathan harshly.

Between gasps the man managed: "Go to—hell."

"Tell us the plane's destination." Jonathan began hammering the man's ribs, sending waves of pain throughout his body. "Talk to us, man."

"Go to—hell," the man gasped.

Jonathan jabbed his knuckles into the man's throat. "Tell us what we want to know."

The dispatcher shook his head, gasping for air.

Harry got up from behind the desk and joined Jonathan. "You don't have to tell us, mister," said Harry calmly. "But of course, it could be voluntary. Without coercion. Naturally, some guys are more voluntary than others. Something to do with the kidneys, they tell me. I know guys of the not-so-voluntary type who had to go to the can every fifteen minutes for years after they got voluntary. Can't seem to hold water, mister."

The man ran the tip of his pink tongue along his lips.

Harry went on. "Then there are guys with ruptured spleens, damaged livers. Like punch-drunk fighters who have stopped too many with their bellies."

Red spots the size of half dollars glowed dully on the man's cheeks.

"We could do lovely business with you, mister," said Harry softly.

"What do you say, mister?" said Jonathan.

The man spat in Jonathan's face. The muscles alongside Jonathan's jaw rippled. "You fuckin' Nazi!" His fist crashed into the man's kidney. He collapsed.

Harry pulled him up against the transmitter panel. The Nazi's eyes came open; bloody.

Jonathan put his knuckles to the man's throat. "You have five seconds. Then I'll rip your throat open."

The dispatcher saw in Jonathan's eyes that he meant it. Barely above a whisper he said, "Lake George."

"Where in Lake George?"

"I don't know. I swear it!"

The knuckles pressed harder.

"I swear to God I don't know. All I know there's a meeting. Where, they didn't tell me."

"Does the pilot work for Marley?"

"Yes."

"When will he be back?"

"In a couple of hours—the most."

They waited for the pilot. He couldn't add anything

to what the dispatcher had told them. Except that at the airfield at Lake George General Marley and Wagner were met by a Mercedes and driven off. Destination unknown. Harry was convinced he was telling the truth.

Before they left, they ripped out the phone, put the transmitter out of commission and with the dispatcher's gun shot out the tires of the jet. The pilot stood by, numb with fear.

A present for the Nazis from David Ring.

David slept.

Never had he experienced sexual ecstasy wrought with such consummate skill. Rabid yet erogenously tender. She had found zones he never knew he possessed. She had raised him to the apogee of pleasure and kept him there until he was about to explode with a mixture of pain and exhilaration. Then with a savage cry she had released him.

He had shuddered.

He had sighed.

"You fantastic bitch!" he had called her.

Now, Anna removed the hypodermic syringe from her handbag, tested it carefully and injected enough of the contents into David's upper arm to keep him sleeping.

She replaced the syringe in her handbag, and took the bag with her to the study.

She removed a sheet of David's personal stationery from a desk drawer and rolled it into the typewriter. *She then proceeded to type a letter to Major Benn Yussid, Israeli Secret Service, Jerusalem, Israel.*

Finished, she unrolled the letter from the typewriter and placed it on the desk.

From her handbag, she took out the minicamera,

focused the desk light on the letter, and proceeded to photograph it.

Then she tore up the letter, put the pieces in her handbag and turned off the desk lamp.

She moved quietly to the sitting room and went directly to the bar. The two cocktail glasses remained where they had left them.

She frowned. Which one was his? Then she remembered.

Hers was closest to the telephone.

She wrapped David's glass in a handkerchief and placed it in her bag.

She returned to the bedroom, smiled wistfully at the sleeping figure on the bed. "Sorry, baby," she whispered. "It could have been nice."

She kissed him gently and climbed in beside him.

# 9

## New York City
## Monday

*The pigeons circled to gain altitude, then began their usual morning flight toward their goal.*

They swam nude; cavorting, laughing, loving. He thought of the night before. That wondrous night! Why? Why had they sent her?

Her skin under his hands was like satin. Without a blemish. He lifted her until her breasts touched his mouth, then he let her down slowly and said softly, "You were magical last night."

"It was you, David," she said smiling. "You and that goddamn drink."

"You're half right," he grinned. "The drink was only fruit juice. And you knew it. So that leaves my personal magnetism and your erotomania for my body."

"You . . . !" She attempted a playful swing at him. He caught her hand and gently pulled her close. Suddenly his desire rose; his eyes closed.

Just as suddenly she wanted him. Her hand slid slowly down his stomach until she reached him; and guided him into her.

There was hardly a ripple in the water, so gentle was their undulation. For David, it was an ecstatic episode; for Anna, a worry. She must not become involved. There was work to be done.

They moved in a smooth, serpentine rhythm, their lips locked to each other. Under and out and around they glided.

Porpoises.

Entwined.

A mating ballet. Then: She thrashed her head away, her mouth open, her face filled with a joyous ecstasy that seemed almost starkly painful.

And she cried out. Primal. Ending with a low, moaning sound. "Oh my God, David," she sobbed.

He kissed her eyes; her lashes beaded, not only from the water that clung. He tasted the salty tears.

He tightened his arms around her. *No—don't let the episode end . . . don't let it be just an episode. . . .*

A sudden urge overcame him . . . he'd never let her go . . . no matter what it was that had brought her into his life. . . .

She caught his look and she knew she had him. Mission completed. But her mind reeled, for realization set in. He had *her! And she wanted it that way. No!*

"I have a meeting," she heard him telling her. "But we'll have lunch at noon. At 21. And I'll tell you how much I love you."

*No!*

"More ways than Elizabeth Barrett Browning could count."

*No!*

She climbed out of the pool and David watched, his heart pounding. Out of control.

*Danger.*

Anna entered Fredericks' apartment. "I got what I could," she said, crossing to him. "I hope they're good ones." Her face was empty of expression. She removed the handkerchief-wrapped cocktail glass from her handbag and handed it to the thin, nervous FBI official.

Fredericks carefully examined it.

"Will the lab really be able to lift the prints?" she asked. There seemed to be a hope in her voice that it could not be done.

Fredericks nodded. "Lift them and transfer them to whatever we wish."

She handed him the minicamera.

"I took the photograph of the letter." She snapped her bag shut. "I've got to go. I'm meeting him for lunch."

"Good work, Anna," said Fredericks. "I suggest that you break it off now that we've got what we want."

Her eyes clouded. *Let him go . . . to be destroyed?*

# Lake George
# Monday

The activity in the cellar of the country mansion was frenzied. Time was crucial. At both sides of a long table men were fashioning tiny cylinders made of thin metal foil. Copper threads extended from their tops like insects' antennae. Other men were packing the finished cylinders with a clear gummy substance.

Another group began placing in position an enormous sheet of what appeared to be glass. So clear and so constructed as to render it virtually invisible. Perplax.

Wagner was impressed though puzzled as he surveyed the work. He turned to General Marley. "Without special percussion it is useless, correct?"

Marley, a tall man, nearly six-four, with a grizzled countenance, grinned. "Watch." At his signal a vicious Doberman on a leash was led to him and commanded to sit.

On the other side of the clear Perplax a man strapped a cat to a stanchion.

Marley released the Doberman with the command: "Get him!"

The Doberman rushed for the cat but crashed headlong into the Perplax screen.

Marley kept his grin. "That's one form of percussion. Unloaded, of course."

Wagner's eyes widened; his thoughts crowding. "*Gott im himmel,*" he murmured.


## *The Conference Room*
## *Monday*

"The only event, David," said Myrna, "that could possibly affect you is the arrival of Yassim Sivad on Friday. Nothing else."

His mind throbbed thinking of Anna. *He loved her. Terribly. How was it possible? What was it, only twenty-four hours? It seemed like . . . always. And*

*she loved him. He saw all the signs. He'd get her
away from the Wagner group.*

"David. . . ?"

*And she'd tell him everything. What the conspiracy
was. The plot . . . my God, was that why he wanted
her? Was that the reason? No. This was a deep,
emotional experience. More important than . . .*

"David. . . ?"

He shook himself alert. "I'm sorry, Myrna. I was . . .
thinking. What were you saying?"

Myrna frowned. She paused, then repeated her
statement that Sivad's arrival on Friday was the only
event that could possibly affect him.

"How?" David was back to reality.

"Let's assume there's a conspiracy against you by
Wagner and company to get you out of the way in
order to give his Nazis a clear field. If they assassinate
Sivad and manage to frame you as lord high execu-
tioner . . ." She spread her hands indicating that the
rest was obvious.

"There are other Nazi-haters around besides me,"
David pointed out. "Jews and non-Jews alike."

"But not as powerful as David Ring."

"I don't go along," said Harry, folding his freckled
hands on the conference table. "Killing Sivad would
make David a hero in the eyes of a lot of people."

Jonathan kept shaking his head. "There's going to
be a frame, all right. But it's something bigger than
just knocking off Sivad and laying the blame on
David."

"Like . . . ?"

"Don't ask me what." The husky black man
shrugged.

David eyed his group. "How is it no one has mentioned the Arabs? Are they in on the frame? Would
they sacrifice Sivad to get to me? Is that why they

handed Wagner ten million dollars? I'm not that important to them. To Wagner, yes. . . . You're right, Myrna. Eliminate me and Wagner has eliminated an obstacle. But where do the Arabs fit in?"

Silence.

David went on. "All right. I'm framed for the murder of Sivad. But, as Harry said, in the eyes of a lot of people I'd be a hero. The Arabs hate me for other reasons. They don't like my close connection with Israel. But . . . hate me ten million dollars' worth?" He shook his head. "The price is too high. No. Wagner's plan goes deeper. He wants me alive for other reasons than what we've discussed here."

He turned to Lipman. "You're thinking, Lippy. Talk to us."

Lipman removed the pipe from his mouth. "Why don't we put Wagner away?"

"We don't put people away, Lippy."

"I meant, send him back to Berlin with something to remember us by."

"It isn't just Wagner, Lippy," David scowled. "There are other people in high places involved. You know that. I have no choice but to assume that whatever the plot is it's tied in with Sivad's visit. What do we do, protect him?"

From Harry: "I've said it before. Let's stop him."

"When? Before his arrival? Impossible. After? Then the die has already been cast. No. We've got to bust the plot wide open within the next four days."

Lipman puffed on his pipe for a moment. Finally he said, "Four days doesn't give us much time."

David grinned. "Look what Israel did in six." He looked at his watch. "I have a lunch date."

He left them sitting there. It wasn't like him, thought Myrna, to leave without some instructions.

Especially during a critical period. She knew what had to be done.

"Harry, Jonathan," she began. "Get started for Lake George. You might get lucky." Her eyes clouded. "Lippy, I'm worried about David."

# 10

## New York City
## Monday

In the fingerprint archives an operator sat at a sorting machine, the cards flipping until it reached the match he was looking for.

The operator called Myrna and told her what he had. She thanked him and said: "You've got five big ones coming, George."

Myrna hung up, then immediately lifted the receiver again and touched the buttons for a number. A man by the name of Larry answered.

"Here's a goody for you, Larry." She read from her notes. "Anna Thornton. Social Security number 557-76-9246. I need a copy of her income tax return and whatever else you can dig up." She listened for a moment, then smiled. "I know it's illegal, Larry. So is murder. If we can stop a major crime by committing a minor one . . . the choice is obvious, right? Besides, I'm about to bribe you. Which is also illegal. So is spitting in the subway, overtime parking, and all those little donations we sprayed you with which you never declared. *N'est-ce pas?*"

Larry apparently saw the logic. "I need it fast." Myrna said. "No later than Thursday morning."

Myrna checked her watch, then returned to the push buttons on the phone.

No one lingered around David's booth at 21. It was a rule never broken.

Anna drained the last of the Cointreau then closed her eyes and recited: "Love is the part, love is the whole. Love is the robe and love is the pall. Ruler of heart and brain and soul, Love is the Lord and slave of all."

David took her hand. "George Macdonald, first stanza, 'A Lover's Thought of Love'."

She smiled. "Is there anything you don't know?"

"I don't know who you are." He gave her a sober look. "Why you came to me, your connection with Wagner."

Silence. Her eyes studied his face.

"Want to tell me?" he said softly.

She couldn't get herself to speak. Say anything. Tell a lie.

"I'll listen," continued David.

Silence. Her lower lip trembled.

"All right. Then you listen. Confession: I have never been told that I was loved." His face became wistful. "Is it enough to be loved without being told? How is one to know?"

"Whom have *you* loved, David?" Her voice soft, tender. "Whom have you told?"

She got her answer after a long wait. "No one . . . until now."

"No!"

He was surprised at her outburst.

Her mind raced. She brought her face close to his. "I love you, David." It was a whisper. "But I don't want you to get hurt. Please—don't love me back."

"They can't hurt me, my darling. Whatever you're caught up in, it doesn't matter. We'll beat them. We'll do it together."

He brushed a wisp of dark hair away from her face. "What are you thinking?"

*Too late.* A look of anguish. A moan.

"What is it?"

*Trapped. No escape. For both of us.* A dazed look.

"Anna!" Sharply.

Then, with firm resolution, she got hold of herself. "I don't know what's come over me, David. But I'm all right now."

"Sure?"

She nodded. "I'm fine. You want to know what my connection is with Wagner?"

David waited.

"None whatsoever. My connection is with Carl Fredericks as special investigator. I was to meet with Wagner who would fill me in with the details of my assignment." She gave him a wry smile. "Which was to lure you into revealing your plans with regard to the coming visit of Sivad. I told him I didn't think it could be done in so short a time . . . I'm good," she grinned, "but not that good. I was lucky. Your coming to the apartment—Hoffman's murder—made it easy for me to make contact. I knew you didn't buy my 'hooker' story, but it got me an invitation. Now all I had to do was . . ." She shrugged. "What

I did. So what happened? I blew the whole thing sky high because I fell in love with you."

David gazed at her hard and long. Finally: "Why do Fredericks and Wagner want to know what I planned to do about Sivad?"

"I don't know."

"Why are they interested in Sivad?"

She shook her head.

"Do you know anything about a meeting in Lake George?"

"No."

He took her hand in both of his. "Forgive me, darling, but it's important that I ask these questions."

"Anything, David." Her mind whirled. Her answers came as if programmed.

"Any connection between Wagner and our secretary of state?"

"I don't know."

"Senator Franklyn?"

She shrugged.

"Reverend Carson?"

"I don't know him."

"Have you ever seen Fredericks together with General Marley?"

"No."

"One last question, darling."

"Yes, David?"

"In the apartment—when you were hiding in the bedroom, you overheard Wagner saying he had plans for me, and that he had a reason to keep me alive. Do you know what he meant?"

"I remember hearing him say it. I have no idea what it was about."

He put her hand to his lips. "You know something, my darling? . . . I believe you."

A sharp intake of breath. *Finito.*

*Why am I trembling?* she asked herself.

The phone beside the table rang. David lifted the receiver. He smiled warmly at Anna.

"Yes?"

Myrna replied: "Your playmate makes her home in Washington, D.C. She's on the president's personal payroll. Keeps an apartment at the Carlyle here in Manhattan. Formerly, she was secretary to Senator Franklyn. Before that, sub-rosa fund raiser for Reverend Carson's Freedom Movement. I'll have more information when I get her income tax return . . . I thought you should know."

Silence. Both ends.

"David. . . ?" Myrna began.

"Thank you," said David just above a whisper. He let the receiver drop in its cradle. *He shuddered. So close. It might have been havoc. . . . A beautiful lady. A love short-lived. A pity.*

Anna eyed him closely, her guard up. "Anything wrong, David?"

He laughed derisively. "Everything." He got up and took her arm. "Let's go pack your things. You're moving in with me."

"What?"

"You're not safe running around loose." He gave her a searching look.

Anna stared back at him. She knew it was over.


# Lake George
# Monday Afternoon

Harry and Jonathan went directly to the Motor Vehicle Bureau. Only five Mercedes sedans were recorded. They interviewed the five registered owners.

Zero.

Harry remembered Fredericks' voice on the tape: *Plan to spend the night.* Hotel? Someone's home? Whose?

Where do we go from here?

# New York City
# Monday Afternoon

Anna's apartment in the Hotel Carlyle on Madison Avenue was expensive. David wondered. Paid for by the president of the United States?

*The president involved with Klaus Wagner and company?*

If so . . . my God, how many more in high places!

David sat in the living room of Anna's suite, surrounded by packed suitcases. A terrifying thought prodded his mind: Insurrection!

Anna came out of the bedroom with an armful of dresses on hangers. She tossed them on the sofa, her expression grim. "I don't relish being kidnapped," she'd told David.

And David had said, "It's for your own protection."

"I can take care of myself."

"Like when you came racing out of Fredericks' apartment in panic, pleading for my help?"

"I told you I made up that story," she retorted.

They hadn't spoken during the packing. Now she glowered at him, about to speak, thought better of it and returned to the bedroom.

She started to close the door when David called out for her to leave it open. She swung the door back open, her jaw tight. Her eyes darted to the phone on the night table. No. Then she remembered. There was a phone in the bathroom. David was careless.

She slipped into the bathroom and made a call. "Carl . . . Anna. David Ring is on to me. Don't ask me how. He's moving me into the penthouse."

Fredericks listened grimly. Then he said: "Most likely he intends to go to work on you with drugs. Sit tight. I'll have someone get him with a tranquilizer dart. I'll have a car waiting for you. Play it cool. Don't change your attitude. Stall as long as you can without arousing his suspicion. I'll need enough time to set it up. Okay? . . . Good girl."

Fredericks hung up, then quickly dialed. It rang for one full minute before the receiver on the other end was lifted.

Fredericks said: "Mr. President . . . ?"

Two bellhops wheeled Anna's luggage and clothing to a waiting cab outside the hotel. David and Anna were close behind.

Traffic was heavy. Anna wondered where it would happen. Most likely in front of the Ring Building. Or here? The cab driver? Too soon.

David supervised the placing of the luggage in the trunk while Anna sat in the cab. David soon joined her and the cab pulled away.

The drive was slow. The passengers silent.

Thoughts:

ANNA: *The phone call in 21.*

DAVID: *On the president's payroll. In what capacity?*

ANNA: *How could he know about me?* She gave him a longing look. There was still time. He would protect her. Oh God . . . too late.

DAVID: *The conspiracy. Nationwide. Worldwide? How to stop -it. Need information. Anna. We'll get it from Anna.*

The cab pulled up to the curb in front of David's apartment building. David and Anna emerged while the driver opened the trunk and began unloading the luggage. David helped him place the bags on the sidewalk.

Anna stood waiting, her dark eyes searching the area.

Down the street a car was parked at the curb. A man behind the wheel. The motor running.

At the revolving doors to the lobby, people were entering and leaving.

A man stood alongside one of the doors, staring in the direction of the cab.

"Stay with the bags," David told the driver. "I'll have someone come down and pick them up. He'll pay you."

David took her arm and led her to the entrance. When they reached the revolving door the man moved away.

They started to cross the lobby; Anna's eyes darting, searching. The guard at the information booth nodded as they passed.

The elevators were discharging and taking on passengers; the armed operators stood stiffly at attention. All these people. It could be any one of them.

*The guard in front of the penthouse elevator?*

"Who are you?" said David frowning. "Where's Frank?"

Anna drew her breath sharply.

"He reported in sick," said the guard. "The agency said it was for one day. May I see some identification, sir?"

"There are only two people who can get that elevator door open." David removed the code card from his pocket. "One is Mr. Lipman; the other . . ."

He inserted the card in the slot in the wall and the door slid open.

"Sorry, sir," said the guard.

"Now may I see *your* identification?" said David frowning.

"Certainly, sir."

The guard reached into his pocket—Anna stiffened —and came up with a leather card case.

David examined it, found it authentic and handed it back.

"Did you report to Mr. Lipman when you came on duty?"

"Yes, sir. At noon."

It had to be him, thought Anna. What is he waiting for?

David ushered Anna into the elevator. He turned his back and inserted the card in the slot to send the elevator up.

Before the door closed, the guard whipped out a gun with a silencer and sent *two bullets into Anna. A look of surprise and anguish contorted her face as the door shut.*

David caught her before she reached the floor. With his free hand he quickly pressed the alarm button and at the same time flipped a switch to send the elevator back down.

"David . . ." gasped Anna. ". . . forgive me. . . ." Lake . . . George . . . look . . ."

She lapsed into unconsciousness.

In the lobby the sound of the alarm was shrill and constant. The crowd stood frozen.

*All areas of egress were immediately sealed off.*

The elevator operators with drawn guns fanned out, searching.

David emerged from the elevator with Anna in his

arms. He transferred her to one of the operators. "Get her upstairs to the hospital. Notify Mr. Lipman."

The alarm sound halted abruptly and an automated voice announced: "Attention, everyone. Attention. Please stay where you are. The doors will be opened shortly."

An operator hurried to David. "He's over by the doors. He has a hostage. Vera Harkavy—Accounting."

Together they threaded their way through the crowd until they reached the killer. He stood behind the woman, an arm around her neck, a gun at her head.

"Open the doors, Mr. Ring," he said. "She doesn't have much time."

"Are you all right, Mrs. Harkavy?" David eyed her anxiously.

She gave him a wan smile. "I'm okay."

"Open the doors," repeated the killer.

"Let her go," said David. "If you pull that trigger we'll kill you on the spot."

"Right. But this lady's life is more important to you than mine. It's not a very good trade, Mr. Ring."

"That's true. What do you suggest?"

"Open the doors. Give me five minutes and I'll let the lady go unharmed."

"No deal."

The killer's face tightened. "If you don't value *her* life, how about yours?"

"I value it."

"Enough to let me go?"

David stared.

The killer could read nothing in David's expression. "I can get off two shots," the killer said, "before your man hits me. One for the lady and one for you."

David wanted the man alive. He needed some

answers. He felt that this was no ordinary hit man; but part of the organization.

*If so, his own life was in no danger.*

David turned to the armed operator. "The minute he kills me open the doors and let him go free." He turned back and noted the killer's confused look. "Your orders," he explained, "were not to touch me, right? Can you imagine what they'll do to you when they find out what happened?" To the operator he said: "Have the engineers open the doors."

The operator nodded and left. David continued. "Fifteen minutes after you're gone every news broadcast will carry the story that David Ring was murdered and his body destroyed. I'll go underground, and that leaves you at the mercy of Klaus Wagner and company."

Beads of sweat appeared on the killer's forehead, his face turned ashen, his body rigid. "You're bluffing," he said hoarsely.

"Am I?"

The doors swung open. David smiled and turned to leave.

"Wait!"

David looked at him questioningly.

"What's the deal?" the killer asked. The hand that held the gun began to tremble.

"If Anna Thornton lives you'll probably get five years. If she dies . . ." David shrugged. ". . . about fifteen." Then he added, "After we get some answers, of course."

The killer weighed the alternative. It wasn't good. He'd be a walking corpse. David Ring was right. His orders were not to harm him. He was safer here.

He released the lady and handed the gun over.

Lipman was waiting for them in the hospital foyer.

He told David that Anna never regained consciousness; that he hadn't as yet notified the police.

"Time for that," said David. "After we get through with this baby."

A nurse came over. "Telephone for you, Mr. Ring."

"Take him to the interrogation room, Lippy. I'll be there in a minute.

David took the phone.

The interrogation room was small, square and brightly lit. There was a table, a few chairs and a cot. A tape recorder sat on the table.

The killer lay on the cot, one sleeve rolled up. A doctor stood over him, rubbing an area of the arm with cotton swabbed in alcohol. He filled a syringe, then gave it a test squirt.

Lipman watched as the doctor carefully injected the solution into the killer's arm.

"He'll be under in three minutes," said the doctor. "You can rely on his statements."

"How long will the serum last?"

"Two hours. If you need more answers I'll give him another shot."

"Good enough."

The doctor pocketed the empty syringe and the solution. "I'll be in the lab if you need me."

Lipman nodded and turned his attention to the man on the cot. "How do you feel?"

"Shitty."

"Better than having Wagner feed you your testicles."

The doctor passed David, who was on the phone. *The doctor was not going to the lab. The lab was in the other direction. He took the elevator down.*

David replaced the phone and went directly to the interrogation room. He poked his head in the door:

"I'm leaving for Washington. I'll be back late tonight or early tomorrow morning. Get me some good answers on that tape."

"Will do."

"Shalom."

Lipman started the tape rolling.

# 11

## Washington, D.C.
## Monday Night

Only one window in the Israeli Embassy showed light.

Ambassador Dubin sat in his study waiting David's
arrival.

Over six feet in height, Dubin's dress and bearing
gave him the look of an aristocrat. His cheeks were
thinned by two parallel folds; his piercing eyes had
an air of intense absorption in some secret worry. He
moved slowly because of a steel brace on one leg.
A victim of the Six-Day War.

David was ushered in and they greeted each other
with a warm embrace. No time was wasted on amenities.

On the desk was a tape recorder with built-in

speaker. The ambassador pressed the start button, and the tape began winding slowly.

David leaned forward to listen.

"To David Ring from Major Benn Yussid of the Israeli Secret Service." He spoke with a clipped British accent. "It is Monday night in Washington. Yassim Sivad, as you well know, will arrive at the U.N. Friday morning. What worries us here at the Mossad is the presence of Klaus Wagner in New York at a time that coincides with Sivad's visit.

"Our information, though sparse, spells a definite peril, not only to Israel, but to Jews around the world. The exact nature of which we have thus far been unable to discover.

"What is further disturbing is that your Secretary of State Brandon has personally arranged for Sivad's presence at the U.N. and has been secretly in contact with Klaus Wagner."

David nodded to the ambassador, indicating he'd known of it.

"In addition," the tape went on, "we know that Wagner's Nazi agents have infiltrated the FBI, the CIA and the Justice Department. We are unable to expose them for we do not possess the physical evidence.

"We sense a coup d'etat in the wind, preceded by a holocaust and destruction of frightening proportions.

"The fuse is lit and it burns shorter as the time of Sivad's visit nears. It calls for action, David. Sivad's appearance at the U.N. must be stopped. And Wagner must be eliminated. Our agents in New York are pinned down and unable to act. Your organization is equipped to do this.

"David—I beg of you—keep Sivad away from the U.N. and see to it that Wagner is destroyed. Please!

*Before it is too late!"* Major Benn Yussid's voice trembled as he signed off with: *"Shalom, David."*

Ambassador Dubin switched off the tape, then gazed questioningly, hopefully, at David, who remained thoughtful.

*Holocaust? Destruction of frightening proportions? A coup d'etat here in these United States?*

*Instigated by a crackpot? And a fanatical terrorist? Yet, there was Secretary of State Brandon. No fanatic. No crackpot. And all those others.*

The ambassador's soft voice broke in. "Well, David?"

David shuddered. "Most of what Major Yussid said I'm aware of. His conclusions are alarming." He shook his head. "I don't think we'll be able to stop Sivad. And so far as destroying Wagner . . . that's not my way."

"But there are no alternatives, David."

"We're working on some, Jacob."

"You might be too late."

David was disturbed because he had no ready answers. Just a dogged, stubborn game plan that guaranteed nothing. What if Major Yussid was right and there would be a holocaust if he did not act? He scowled. Damn!

"Jacob," he began. "Assume we stopped Sivad and wasted Wagner, do you think that would be the end of the Nazi movement? When such people as Secretary Brandon, General Marley and Senator Franklyn are involved? And all those others we don't know about?" He stood up and walked to the window. "How many secret Nazis do you suppose are out there? In the House—in the Senate; the Pentagon—the armed forces?"

He returned to face the ambassador. "Jacob, the only sure way to kill a snake is to chop his head off.

There are ten *Wagners* ready to step in for each one we eliminate. All backed by the Arab bloc. What do we gain?"

"Time," said the ambassador softly.

"And new enemies," added David. "No, Jacob, we must expose whatever plot is brewing and those connected with it. Only then can we shatter the movement."

"And if you are unable to accomplish this, David?"

"I have four days."

"And if at the end of four days you are unsuccessful?"

David became lost in his thoughts, searching for an answer. "Then it's God's will," he said finally.

"As it was at Belsen and Auschwitz?"

David wasn't sure. His face creased with pain. "How else can you explain that happening?"

"God had nothing to do with it!" exclaimed Dubin angrily. "It is sheer blasphemy to blame Him for the Holocaust." He stood up and waved a finger. "And if there should be another at this time because of your failure to act, would you still maintain that God willed it?"

"Who, then, the devil?" he retorted. "If so, then it's your contention that the devil has more power than the Lord."

"Or," said the ambassador bitterly, "that he is doing the Lord's work."

"Let's stay with reality, Jacob," he said kindly. "We must consider three quantities. *Where, when and what*. *Where*, we must assume is at the U.N. *When*—Friday. *What* is the unknown quantity. The information I have indicates that I'm in the middle of what they are planning." He gave the ambassador a wan smile. "Major Benn Yussid didn't know that, did he?"

"I don't understand," said the ambassador. "What do you mean, you're in the middle?"

"I'm both the subject and object of their conspiracy—whatever it is. For some reason, they've got to trap me. Otherwise they lose." He stood up. "Send a message to Benn Yussid. Tell him we'll do everything in our power to abort Wagner's scheme. Tell him we may already have achieved a breakthrough. We have one of Wagner's men under drug interrogation. I'll keep in touch."

David left.

The ambassador sighed heavily.

*On the wall in the ambassador's study, concealed in the contemporary design of a menorah and unknown to the ambassador, was a bug.*

*In a cellar nearby, a man lifted a pair of earphones from his head and removed a reel of tape from a machine.*

# 12

## New York City
## Monday—Midnight

All during the flight back from Washington, David's mind was in a turmoil. Major Benn Yussid was not given to fancy. His message was a grave warning; heavy with portent. Perhaps Wagner *should* be destroyed; and Sivad stopped. But then wouldn't Israel be blamed? More ammunition against the Jews.

No. He'd do it his way. The key was at Lake George—Anna's last words. Harry and Jonathan would find something; and . . . the killer in the hospital spilling his guts on tape . . .

The killer lay on the cot in the interrogation room, a sheet covering his body.

"Cardiac arrest," explained Lipman. "Before I could get anything out of him."

With a cry of anguish, David struck the wall with his fist.

"Doctor Frankel," continued Lipman, "shot him with an O.D. of potassium chloride instead of the serum. We've got tracers out for him. He won't get far, David."

"I want him alive," said David grimly.

"Those were the orders."

At Kennedy International Airport, a stocky, somewhat rumpled man, Doctor Frankel, carrying an attaché case, left his cab and hurried into the International Terminal.

He hastened along a passageway that led to the waiting room, nervously eyeing the people moving with him and toward him. A sign directed him to gate 5. Soon he would be safe.

There were not many people in the waiting area. Good. A crowd would be dangerous. He suddenly felt an overpowering desire to urinate. He hurried into the men's room. It was empty.

He stood at a urinal relieving himself when a man entered. Frankel glanced at him sharply; a feeling of panic seized him. He swung the attaché case under his arm and reached inside his jacket for his pistol. He wouldn't be taken. No.

The man stood at a wash basin combing his hair. Frankel sensed he was being watched in the mirror. Should he turn around to face him? He kept his hand on the gun under his jacket; his other hand zipped up his pants. Now he transferred the attaché case and started for the door. If the man made a move . . .

The man turned for the door at the same moment. Frankel got off two shots in rapid succession.

The man's mouth fell open; a look of surprise on his face. He sank to the floor. "Why?" he was able to gasp.

The waiting area was beginning to fill. Frankel looked about him wildly; praying no one heard the shots or saw him leave the men's room. He was sure the man he'd killed was one of David Ring's agents. He sat down, holding the attaché case between his knees. He checked his watch. Should be boarding time any minute.

A tiny, doll-like woman took a seat next to him, opened her handbag and removed some unfinished lace attached to a shuttle, and began tatting. Her handbag fell from her lap.

Frankel stooped to retrieve it. She thanked him.

"Attention, please," said the voice over the public address system. "Brazilian Airlines flight seventy-nine now boarding at gate five."

The tiny lady replaced the tatting in her handbag, rose, smiled at Frankel and headed for the boarding gate.

Frankel slowly keeled over, a knife protruding from his side.

# 13

## New York City
## Tuesday

U.N. Plaza was teeming.

Schoolchildren, carrying their lunch bags, were disgorged from buses, while teachers struggled to keep them in line. A bored tour director droned the history of the U.N. to his avid listeners. A company of nuns chattered as they moved toward the entrance. Indian women in colorful saris mingled with swarthy men wearing turbans.

Assorted sounds.

*Then came the pigeons.*

*As they neared the plaza they began their descent until they were directly above it. Then without breaking speed they swooped down, wheeled and took off, heading southwest.*

It was a motley assemblage that gathered in David Ring's conference room. Men and women of all sizes and shapes and colors. Some were bedraggled; others could be mistaken for bankers, prostitutes, bookies. There were prim-looking women and elderly men. An assortment of humanity in disguise.

They lined the walls listening intently as David grimly briefed them.

"Time is running out," David told them. "We had a lead in Lake George but Harry and Jonathan unfortunately came up empty. No fault of their own. They were working in a vacuum.

"Three of Wagner's agents were destroyed before we could question them. Right now we need a connection, anybody who's had any kind of contact with a member of Wagner's company. Unlimited funds, as you know, are at your disposal.

"Fredericks, Reverend Carson, Wagner have disappeared. Probably holed up somewhere around Lake George. Senator Franklyn, Secretary Brandon are not in Washington. General Marley hasn't been at the plant for a week. If you should find any one of them, don't hesitate to bring him in.

"Each of you has under his or her command ten workers. I want all of you to descend on Lake George. Let the townspeople know what you're looking for. Someone will hit the panic button and lead us to the hideout.

"Check the homes near and around the lake. Look for anything that might arouse your suspicion. Keep an eye out for a Mercedes sedan. Our only hope is to discover their meeting place. Once we do we'll find enough clues around to break the strike. You have Wednesday and Thursday. Friday might be too late.

"Myrna, put the heat on your IRS contact. Anna Thornton's tax return is important.

"Harry, I want you and Jonathan to strip Fredericks' apartment to the bare bones.

"All of you—get your sleep in now. Because you'll be without it for the next seventy-two hours."

He gave them a warm smile. "God bless you."

They filed out silently.

# 14

## New York City
## Wednesday

It rained.
*Yet, the pigeons were released.*
*The usual objective.*

## Lake George, N.Y.

Two agents, Miller and Elster, working as a team, spotted the Mercedes. It was parked in front of a large, three-storied shingled dwelling. A wrought iron sign planted in the lawn at the entrance, spelled out: BENEVITO GAGLIANO, M.D.

They parked on the opposite side of the street and waited. It was agreed one would tail the Mercedes; the other would see what the doctor might have to offer.

A man wearing a chauffeur's cap came out of the house, started the motor of the Mercedes and kept it running.

Soon, a second man, his head swathed in bandages, wearing dark glasses and a hat pulled low, came out of the house and entered the Mercedes. It drove off.

Miller began the tail. Elster crossed the street toward the entrance to the house.

A hard-looking strawberry blonde behind a frail, spindly desk offered Elster a cold look as he came in.

"Lieutenant Elster, New York City Police Department," he said, flashing a fake I.D. "I'd like to see the doctor, please."

Elster looked like a cop, husky and clean-cut with a businesslike demeanor.

Doctor Gagliano expressed surprise at being visited by a New York policeman. He was a bald-headed man of about sixty, dressed in a white smock. He wore thick, rimless glasses.

Elster wondered why there were no patients around.

"Homicide investigation," said Elster, taking a seat. "The patient who just left is a suspect. What can you tell us about him?"

The doctor spread his hands. "I know nothing about him except that he came here for treatment."

"What sort of treatment?"

"Why, lieutenant," he said with a hurt look. "You know I'm not at liberty to reveal that. You must have heard of the sanctity of the doctor-patient relationship."

The sarcasm wasn't lost on Elster. "Then would you give me his name and address."

The doctor eyed him curiously. "You traced him here. Why didn't you ask him directly?"

"I didn't want to lose him. He might have told me I had no jurisdiction."

"I might tell you the same thing." The doctor gave him a cold stare.

Elster wondered how much force he'd have to use to get him to talk. On the other hand, it might not be necessary; Miller had probably gotten the answers by now. But just in case . . .

"I can't give you any more time," said Gagliano abruptly. He stood up.

Elster got out of the chair and put out his hand. "Hope I haven't inconvenienced you."

The doctor shook it perfunctorily. "Not at all," he said, a slight curl on his lip.

Elster spun him around, twisting the doctor's arm in a painful hammerlock behind his back.

The doctor's face twisted in pain. He emitted a stifled scream.

"I need some answers, doctor," said Elster. "If you play games with me, I'll not only break your arm, I'll pull it out of your shoulder. Question: Who was the patient?"

Pause.

A sharp tug. A cry.

Answer: "Klaus Wagner."

"What did you do for him?"

"Skin graft on his forehead . . . to eliminate a scar. . . ."

"Now give me the address . . . You'd better be right."

"Nineteen Mill Road. For chrissake, take it easy!"

"Sure." Elster lifted the phone with his free hand. "What's the number down there?"

"It's 3-8736."

From memory, thought Elster. Must use it often.

With his free hand he dialed the number. Then: "Hello—this is the phone company. We've had a mix-up on the lines. Is this Nineteen Mill Road? . . .

Thank you." He shifted the phone to his shoulder and pressed the receiver button.

After he dialed the number again he said in a disguised voice: "Has Klaus gotten back yet?" He listened. "I'll call him later. Thanks."

He dropped the phone and released the doctor's arm. "You were a good boy, doc." Elster yanked the wires out of the wall. "A good Nazi. I ought to kill you. Some other time, maybe."

Gagliano leaped for the desk drawer; Elster beat him to the gun. He brought it down hard on the doctor's head. The doctor fell onto the desk and slid off onto the floor. He lay still.

In the reception foyer, the blonde grimly watched Elster rip out the telephone lines.

"Better get some ice for the doctor's skull," he said. "He's got a nasty blow."

She made no reply; made no move. Just glared hatred.

Elster started for the door. He heard the first *fttt* and at the same instant felt a sharp pain between his shoulders. He didn't hear the second one. His head exploded.

The blonde, gripping the pistol, with its silencer protruding, looked at Elster splayed out on the floor and smiled.

Miller tailed the Mercedes to 19 Mill Road. He gave it enough time before he peered through the iron grille of the gate. He could see nothing.

The wall was too high to scale; bare of shrubbery that might have given him a footing.

He backed the car up to the gate, clambered up onto the roof and swung himself over the dirt driveway. Miller was small and lithe, his movements quick and agile.

He moved swiftly until he reached the clearing where the cars were parked. There was the Mercedes, parked with a number of others. He made a note of the license number then searched the glove compartment and discovered the electronic device that swung the gate open. He used it. A fast getaway was assured.

With extreme caution, he made his way around to the side of the house. He noticed a slanted cellar door. Two transoms were set in the cement foundation, light spilling from them.

He dropped to his hands and knees and looked inside. A dozen workers were assembling an assortment of electronic devices. Klaus Wagner holding an animated discussion with General Marley. No sounds. A state trooper said something to Wagner. Marley seemed to agree.

Miller felt the gun barrel pressed against the back of his head.

"Don't move," was the biting command. "Get up slowly but don't turn around."

Miller complied. Then moved with lightning speed, a sidewise jerk of the head and a backward thrust of the fist into the groin.

The silenced bullet whistled past his ear and lodged in the wall of the house. Miller's fist caught the point of the guard's jaw. The guard's duties were temporarily suspended.

Miller raced across the grounds to his car, anxious to get out of there and to a phone.

He sped along the deserted highway heading for town. He wondered what was going on in that house on Mill Road. He hoped there'd be time for David to organize a raid.

At first he did not hear the wail of the siren far in the distance. It grew louder; then he saw the car, its lights flashing.

He compressed his lips and shoved down hard on the accelerator. The needle moved forward to ninety; Miller grimly trying to hold the car steady.

No contest.

The state trooper drew abreast of him and fired point blank.

The car swerved, hit a tree and was incinerated.

Miller did not feel the heat.

Harry and Jonathan stripped Fredericks' apartment clean.

Zero.

Reverend Carson's residence.

Zero.

David received word that Elster and Miller had been murdered.

Anything else from Lake George?

Zero . . . so far.

Myrna?

She walked north along Central Park West—the park side. Night. Her IRS man fell in step with her. Without breaking stride he reached into his pocket and handed her an envelope which she placed into her shoulder bag. In return, he received a smaller envelope and they parted.

It was no ordinary mugger who followed Myrna. He was well-dressed; carried a leather briefcase. She didn't sense his presence.

As he got closer, he opened the briefcase and pulled out a knife.

She heard his step, but she kept moving, every muscle tense; her senses tuned to a fine pitch.

Suddenly she wheeled. The steel winked as it caught the street light.

But he was slow and clumsy. She caught his wrist, twisting it expertly inward and down. The knife clattered to the pavement. At the same time she brought her knee up, crushing into the man's groin. He sank, trying to relieve the pressure on his wrist.

It snapped like a chicken bone; his scream could not be heard above the roar of the traffic.

He fell, writhing.

Myrna dug her elbow into his throat. "Who sent you?"

He managed a gasp: "Fredericks."

"How did he know about the envelope?"

He gurgled blood-flecked saliva. "I . . . can't breathe . . ."

She eased up on the pressure. "Talk to me."

"I don't . . . know anything," he managed. "I was to get . . . a thousand dollars."

She left him lying there.

It's dangerous to walk on the park side of Central Park West at night.

They were in David's study; the federal income tax return spread out on the desk.

Anna's gross income was one million, two.

A low whistle from David.

Occupation: personal assistant to the president of the United States.

WAGES: Two hundred thousand per.

SCHEDULES: Stocks. Bonds. Dividends.

Rental from town house, Manhattan.

SECOND TRUST DEEDS:

(a) Apartment buildings, Washington, D.C.

(b) Factory, Lynfrank Electronics, Long Island City, N.Y.

David looked up. "Senator Franklyn's operation." Back to the form.

(c) Reverend Carson's Freedom Church.

FIRST MORTGAGE: American Legion Building, Jersey City, N.J.

SECOND MORTGAGE: Lake Front Property: 19 Mill Road, Lake George, N.Y.

Bingo!

David looked at his watch. "It'll be daylight in an hour. Lippy, call the airfield and have them get our plane ready. Myrna, you want to come along?"

"Try to keep me away," she grinned.

"Lippy," said David, "get on it. Also, we'll need some muscle. Have two cars waiting for us at the Lake George airfield. Probably can get them from Albany. But no drivers. Stick close, Lippy, and mind the store." He turned to the others. "Let's go."

"Good hunting," said Lippy.

## Long Island

A black sedan made its way toward the Techno Chemical plant at high speed. It slowed down as it neared its objective.

The driver and the man seated next to him proceeded to don stocking masks. The driver placed a .45 automatic on his lap while his partner picked up a rifle from the floor.

In the booth at the entrance to the plant, the watchman sat reading a magazine. He looked up as a pair of headlights penetrated. He put his magazine down and stepped out to meet the car.

The rifle was aimed at his head.

He turned and raised his hands as directed.

The driver leaned out and hit him behind the ear with the butt of his pistol.

The partner with the rifle stepped out and signaled the driver to get moving. He then dragged the unconscious form of the watchman into the booth and seated him in the chair.

The car pulled up to the loading platform where it was met by a man holding a large carton. He placed it on the rear seat of the car.

The driver tied the compliant worker to a post, gagged him, then reentered the car. "Okay?" the driver asked.

The man nodded.

Outside the watchman's booth, the driver picked up his partner and drove off.

Several minutes later, the watchman regained consciousness.

The incident was reported to the police.

Because the robbery involved strategic materials, the FBI was notified.

*Fredericks was assigned to the case.*

# 15

## New York City
## Thursday

At the United Nations, one security officer looking up at the April sky said to a fellow officer: "Funny about those pigeons. The way they come around every morning."

"Yeah."

They watched the pigeons swoop down and take off.

"They do that every morning."

"Funny."

"Must be about two dozen of them."

"Yeah."

"And they always go back in the same direction."

"Funny."

They watched until the pigeons disappeared from sight.

"Let's get our coffee."

"Yeah."

## Lake George, N.Y.

The two-engined jet taxied to the administration building and came to a halt. David, Harry, Jonathan and Myrna stepped out, followed by four husky men.

They crossed to a parking area where they were met by a man holding a clipboard.

David signed where indicated and the man directed them to the two cars they were to take.

David and his group entered one car; the musclemen the other.

David drove the lead car with Myrna beside him, a road map in her lap. She directed him to take the secondary road at the next intersection.

They proceeded slowly, then turned onto a rutted dirt road, lined on both sides with shrubs and trees. The signpost read: MILL ROAD.

"We'd better stop," said David, "and walk the rest of the way."

A quarter of a mile farther, they stood in front of the electronic gate. Half of it hung crazily on one hinge; the other was ground into the dirt.

This had to be it. The stone post alongside said it was number 19.

David paused.

*Something had happened here.*

They hurried along the driveway until they reached the parking area.

In the background the lake shimmered.

The air smelled of spent smoke.

David's face collapsed at the sight that greeted him.

*The only thing left standing of the house was the brick chimney and the stone foundation.*

David cried out in anguish. "*They knew we were coming!*"

He strode to the center of the ruins; his body filled with pain. He touched the ground with the palm of his hand. "Still warm," he murmured. "It probably happened last night. After they discovered we were getting close."

The others remained silent, waiting for direction.

"Major Benn Yussid was right," continued David, hushed. "I should have wiped out Wagner when I had the chance."

He faced them, his jaw tight. "Tomorrow we stop Yassim Savid." His voice was low, but intense. "There's not much time left. But we'll give it a try."

Myrna remained behind.

To search.

For what?

# 16

## Camp David
## Thursday

The helicopter had a single passenger. As it approached the compound, the pilot activated the radio with: "This is Bloodstock. Bloodstock calling."

A voice answered: "We receive you, Bloodstock."

"Request permission to land."

"What is your code?"

"Meisterstück."

"Permission granted."

The helicopter descended swiftly and landed in the presence of two armed M.P.'s.

The door flipped open and the passenger disembarked carrying a small valise; he was escorted across the landing pad into one of the buildings.

The president of the United States sat behind the desk in his study, engrossed in his writing. He was a large man, fifty-eight years old, with the build of a college athlete gone to flab. His high forehead gleamed in the light from a desk lamp. His thinning hair was a dull mixture of brown and gray. He wore dark-rimmed glasses for close work.

Charles W. Anderson was president by a fluke. He had been named vice-president by his predecessor only to pay a political debt. Then came the sudden and unexpected death of his mentor and Anderson—Ohio ward heeler and political hack—was elevated to the nation's highest office. He had not risen to the occasion. He knew it; the voters knew it. He had not expected to win the next election. He had even had doubts about whether to embarrass himself by running. But now . . .

He put down his pen and placed the final sheet of paper under a thick pile. He had labored long and hard on this speech and he breathed a sigh of satisfaction. He leaned back and began reading aloud. "My fellow Americans. This morning men's souls were seared by the butchery that took place at the United Nations.

"Bloated with madness and blinded by a paranoiac craving for vengeance, a foreign government struck a terrible, bloody blow against innocent people. Until we have assembled incontrovertible proof, that government shall remain nameless. However, at this very moment . . ."

Klaus Wagner stood in the doorway. "Excuse me, Mr. President . . ."

The president looked up.

"He has just arrived," said Wagner.

"Good. Have him come in." The president rose to greet his visitor.

Lipman crossed briskly and extended his hand. "Mr. President."

"Good to see you, Julius." They shook hands vigorously. "I appreciate your coming." The president looked toward the doorway. "Come in, gentlemen."

They were all there: General Marley, Reverend Carson, Senator Franklyn, Secretary Brandon and Carl Fredericks.

"Forgive me, Charlie," said Lipman, "if I should seem to hurry this meeting. David Ring might return sooner than I expect."

"Of course. Please sit down."

"Thank you." Lipman took a deep breath. "Here's how we stand. A search of the Ring penthouse will reveal traces of the explosive material supposedly stolen from General Marley's plant."

The president nodded.

"Carl has a photograph of a letter typed on Ring's machine addressed to the head of the Israeli Secret Service, implicating him in the conspiracy. Ring's fingerprints have been transferred to the paper."

A look of pain crossed the president's face. "Anna typed that letter, I remember." He closed his eyes. "Anna . . ."

"It had to be done," said Lipman softly.

The president sighed. "I suppose. . . . Please go on."

"Police costumes," continued Lipman, "will be found in the vacant loft building owned by David Ring. They will be identified as stolen merchandise.

"Senator Franklyn had reported that top secret electronic devices were missing from the factory vaults."

"Excellent," said the president.

Lipman bent to open the suitcase. "Now here is something you might find interesting." He removed a tape playback and a cassette. "Last Monday night

David Ring flew to Washington to meet with the Israeli ambassador in the embassy."

He inserted the cassette. "We had the room bugged. This is what transpired."

Lipman pressed the button; the tape rolled.

MAJOR YUSSID'S VOICE: "*To David Ring from Major Benn Yussid of the Israeli Secret Service. It is Monday night in Washington. Yassim Sivad, as you well know, will arrive at the U.N. Friday morning. What worries us here at the Mossad is that Klaus Wagner might expose you and so prevent the holocaust we have planned. The fuse is lit and it burns shorter as the time of Sivad's visit nears. It calls for action, David. Klaus Wagner must be eliminated in order to insure the total destruction of the U.N. Nothing must interfere. Please. I beg you. See to it that Wagner is destroyed. Shalom.*"

AMBASSADOR'S VOICE: "*Well, David?*"

DAVID'S VOICE: "*Send a message to Major Benn Yussid. Tell him not to worry. The U.N. will be destroyed as planned. And as for Wagner, my agents will have him pinned down so that he will be unable to act. Tell him no one can stop us.*"

End of tape. Long silence.

"My God!" breathed the president, awed. "How did you manage it?"

"Electronic genius," said Lipman, grinning.

"Will it stand up?"

Lipman paused, then said: "No."

"What?"

"Not under scientific scrutiny by experts."

The president looked confused. "How do you propose to cure that?"

"Eliminate the experts."

"But at a trial . . ."

"Charlie," interrupted Lipman, "forgive me. The

less you know about the events following the arrest, the better."

"He's right, Charlie," said Fredericks.

The president scowled. "I don't understand. You mean I might not approve?"

"Oh, you will approve," chuckled Wagner.

"If you knew in advance," said Reverend Carson, "you might not be able to summon the right amount of righteous indignation when it happens."

"It calls for spontaneous reaction," said Brandon.

"No offense, Charlie," interposed Marley, "but you're a lousy actor. You're great when taken by surprise. You hit from the crotch. But if you knew in advance, your indignation would sound phony."

The president looked at the group assembled around his desk. The paunchy Lipman, sucking on a cold pipe; General Marley, his lanky frame towering over the others; the thin, nervous Fredericks; blond, muscular Wagner.

Then there was the Reverend Carson, a six-footer but bent, not with age—he wasn't yet fifty. Perhaps with the evil that the president secretly suspected would ride the minister straight into the mouth of Hell someday.

There was Secretary of State Brandon, a smallish fat man, probably bullied and scorned as a schoolboy; he still tended to pout when events got out of hand.

And Senator Franklyn, whose thick head of curly hair and stentorian voice matched in passion the mad gleam in his eyes whenever he harangued his constituents with tales of his own glorious deeds and the wrongs of his enemies. Hitler himself must have squirmed in his grave in envy each time Franklyn mounted the podium.

The president searched all of their faces but found no reassurance.

"I don't know what the hell you're talking about," he growled.

"Trust me, Charlie," said Lipman. He tossed the cassette to Fredericks. "Just pray that nothing goes wrong tomorrow."

"I hope not." The president looked unhappy. Then brightly: "Would you like to hear my speech, Julius?"

"I don't have time, Charlie." He rose. "I won't be seeing you until after the event. Stay well."

"Thanks, Julius."

General Marley and Wagner saw him to the door. "Your moves are brilliant, Julius," said Marley.

Lipman began filling his pipe. "See to it that the vice-president is on the dais when Sivad arrives."

"I mentioned it. He thought it was unusual."

"It's a must. I don't want him around."

"Will do."

Lipman turned to Wagner. "Your cell leaders have been alerted?"

"All over the world," replied Wagner. "The riots will begin right after the president's speech."

They moved out to the helicopter pad. Lipman's face turned wistful. "I still think we could have planned the frame without the slaughter."

Marley grinned. "In a war, civilians have been known to die."

Lipman gave him a cold stare. "Also generals."

# 17

## New York City
## Thursday Afternoon

Lipman sat in the darkness of the confessional, his head bowed, his voice low, vibrant.

". . . . For so many years the jealousy within me has raged to the point that nothing less than his total destruction could bring me peace. And yet, on the eve of my triumph, I sense no relief. Now an overpowering guilt invades my entire being. I have traded one cancer for another."

He paused; sobs shook his frame.

"Go on, my son."

He took a deep breath. "What I have told you, father, are parables. I have omitted names and events so that you would not have to share my burden. They are imbedded in my brain and cannot be cast out.

Pray for my forgiveness, father, though I don't deserve it."

He stumbled out of the booth, pale and shaken. He dropped to his knees, burying his face in his hands.

"Oh, David, David," he sobbed. "What have I done to you! I love you, David . . . I love you . . ."


# New York City
# Thursday Night

Police Captain Peter Hansen stood in the front of David's conference room alongside a diagram set on an easel. David had assembled his agents for one final effort.

He stood in back of the room listening soberly. As did Harry, Jonathan . . . Lipman.

"Sivad's plane will arrive approximately 10 A.M.," the captain was telling them. He indicated with his pointer. "The motorcade will take the parkway here, and then turn onto Queens Boulevard. You can figure that they'll reach the Queensborough Bridge about forty minutes after landing. All traffic will be diverted to the lower level to give the motorcade free access to the upper.

"Once over the bridge they will turn east, then head south until they reach U.N. Plaza."

Hansen, a beefy man with huge hands looked over at David. "Why they decided on the bridge when the Midtown Tunnel would be closer, I can't figure. . . . Dave, I don't know what you have in mind and believe me I don't care to know. But whatever it is, I wish you luck." He put down the pointer. "I think I ought to get the hell out of here."

David came around to the front of the room.
"Thanks, Pete. . . . Harry, take Pete out through the
basement delivery area. I don't want him seen by
anyone." He turned to the group. "It's pretty obvious
that the bridge is where we'll have to bottle him up.
If we stop him . . ."

For a moment he was lost in thought.

"Then—" he added, just above a whisper "—maybe
everything else stops."

*Please God.*

# 18

## New York City
## Friday

The pigeons took off from the rooftop of an unlived-in loft building in lower Manhattan. Tiny metal capsules with threadlike wires attached, circled their necks on a thin chain.

They headed northeast.

The General Assembly Hall of the United Nations was filled. Except the area where the Israeli delegation was to sit.

Vacant.

All members of the Security Council were on the dais. No one was at the lectern.

Reserved for Yassim Sivad.

Outside, lines of grim police secured the area. TV

cameras and crews stood by. Along one side of the perimeter a sullen crowd waited.

Total silence. It was a clear, bright spring day. Not a cloud in the sky.

Across from the plaza, a line of pickets stood behind police barricades listening to a police sergeant on his bullhorn.

The picket signs read:

> YASSIM SIVAD, MURDERER!
>
> SIVAD, THE ASSASSIN!
>
> SIVAD, THE BUTCHER!
>
> SLAYER OF WOMEN AND CHILDREN!
>
> CUTTHROAT!
>
> SLAUGHTERER!
>
> BLOODTHIRSTY KILLER!

"Now hear this," said the sergeant. "I'll only say it once. You are to stay in back of these lines. You are to keep moving. Anyone who thinks he can break through, I tell you right here and now, I'm giving you fair warning, I'll crack anybody's head who tries it.

"For your information, I hate the s.o.b. as much as you do, but Sivad is a guest of the United Nations, and the police force of the city of New York has been assigned the duty to protect him. And that's what we're going to do come hell or high water.

"Talk and shout as much as you want. Yell your lungs out if you feel like. But keep marching in a circle . . . . in a circle . . ."

At a corner of the field in Kennedy International Airport, a line of black Lincoln Continental sedans with uniformed chauffeurs prepared to act as Sivad's cortege. Motorcycle policemen revved their engines.

Arab dignitaries in their native dress watched the 747 with its special passenger taxi to a halt.

The portable stairway was quickly rolled into position.

No firearms were visible.

Yassim Sivad stood on the top step of the stairway for a moment, a grin decorating his unshaven face. He wore his unconventional headdress, a drab uniform and a sidearm.

Still smiling, he hurried down the steps to embrace the dignitaries. He was then quickly ushered into the lead limousine while the rest of the entourage filled the other cars.

The police escort moved out and the motorcade started on its way.

A glazier's truck pulled up at the curb of U.N. Plaza and two officers in special service uniforms got out.

Fastened to the side of the truck was a large, square sheet of what appeared to be glass. It was so clear it offered no reflection.

The two officers unfastened the transparent square, lifted it and carefully placed it on a dolly, then wheeled it toward the entrance.

A policeman on the security line eyed it curiously. "What the hell is that?" he asked his buddy.

His partner shrugged. "Bulletproof glass, I guess."

The object was set into the slot of a wooden base positioned at right angles to the entrance in front of a podium facing the TV cameras. Here Sivad was to address the people of the city; later, in the General Assembly Hall, he was to speak to the world.

At the approaches to the Queensborough Bridge, police were shunting traffic to the lower level. Just as Captain Hansen said they would.

The upper level was deserted. *Except for the painter at work on the top cable near the Queens side.* Two pails were attached to his belt.

On the cable close to the Manhattan side, another painter was at work.

David, at the controls of his helicopter, watched the motorcade proceeding below him.

He reached for his intercom.

"Calling all units. Calling all units."

Harry replied: "This is unit one."

Unit one was a fire truck with full crew in uniform parked near the entrance to the upper level of the bridge on the Queens side. Harry was in the front seat with the driver.

"This is unit two," answered Jonathan from another fire truck at the Manhattan side.

The painters acknowledged they were units three and four.

"Motorcade passing through to Forest Hills," reported David. "Should reach the bridge in fifteen minutes. Stand by. Out."

Harry and his crew prepared to don gas masks.

Jonathan did the same.

The painters removed smoke bombs from their pails.

"Attention all units—motorcades approaching Sunnyside. Five minutes."

Sivad sat between two Arab hosts; his smile frozen in contemplation of his triumph. Soon he would be a world figure. Did not Secretary Brandon promise him that? And Klaus Wagner—his good friend. Such great plans! A surprise stroke, they had told him. At last he would come into his own!

He glanced at his watch. "How much longer?" he asked.

"Ten, fifteen minutes," replied his host.

"Good. Good." He settled back to renew his thoughts, when the phone buzzer sounded.

The Arab picked it up. "Yes?"

He listened; his eyes wide.

David saw the motorcade slow up, then stop. One of the motorcycle policemen turned around and drove up to the lead limousine. From David's point of view it was apparent that he was receiving instructions, for he quickly rejoined his partner and at full speed the entourage swung off the boulevard onto a side street.

Puzzled, David called his units. "Something's up," he said. "The motorcade has left the boulevard and is heading east. I think Sivad has been tipped off. He must be trying for the Midtown Tunnel. Now hear this: Once they gain entrance, I want that tunnel blocked at both ends. Acknowledge."

Harry and Jonathan prepared for the new plan. The units on the bridge cable were informed that the bridge plan was scrubbed and to come down.

Harry's fire engine on the Queens side of the river moved at breakneck speed through traffic, the crew hanging on, its sirens screaming.

Jonathan's engine weaved wildly through the Manhattan traffic toward the tunnel.

The limousines following the motorcycle escort careened through the streets, their tires screeching as they made the turns.

David followed. *What made them change?*

Harry signaled: "Nearing tunnel approach."

David answered: "Pull over and wait for the motorcade to enter. Don't let them see you. Repeat: Don't let them see you. Once they enter the tunnel, proceed immediately to seal them off. Use the tear gas as planned. Over."

"That's a roger."

"Come in Jonathan."

"Two minutes away, Manhattan side."

"Penetrate tunnel wrong way approximately five hundred feet. Use the gas. I want him alive."

"Roger . . . wait a minute . . . what the hell . . ."

"What is it?"

"Pull out! Pull out!"

"Jonathan . . ."

"Oh my God!"

A huge gasoline tank truck, driverless, swung directly in the path of Jonathan's speeding engine. Jonahan started to leap.

A deafening roar. Both vehicles consumed in a great fireball. Including Jonathan and crew.

"Jonathan!" screamed David. "Jonathan! . . ."

Far to the west, David saw a glare of light hit the sky like heat lightning. Smoke rose near the horizon. A few seconds later, sounds like distant thunder reached him.

Horror in his voice. "Jonathan . . . please. God . . ."

David looked down and saw Harry's engine parked at right angles to the tunnel approach.

"Come in, Harry . . ."

Fear gripped him.

"Come in, Harry . . . Harry!"

Just the crackle of static.

The motorcade sped along the approach to the tunnel.

"For God's sake, Harry!"

The limousines disappeared into the mouth of the tunnel.

David jammed viciously at the controls of his craft. It descended rapidly, its rotor blades beating noisily at the air.

He saw Harry's engine, silent, seemingly deserted.

It loomed larger and larger as the helicopter dropped closer.

There it was. All of it. The crew sprawled crazily in their death throes, their bodies bullet-riddled. Harry and the driver . . . their faces half shot away.

"Oh, God!"

Heedless, suicidal, David climbed his helicopter and pointed it for the river, toward Manhattan.

The motorcade burst out of the tunnel at full speed, the police sirens wailing, clearing the way to the U.N.

David, his face ashen, his jaw set, began to descend as he rapidly shortened the distance between himself and the procession.

He was directly above them, preparing to dive.

Sivad's bodyguard, in the second car, leaned out and pointed a Schmeisser automatic pistol at the chopper.

The helicopter staggered under the blast of gunfire; it fell off to the side, its rotors flailing wildly.

David grimaced in pain, his arm hit. He worked furiously at the controls, losing altitude, trying to steer it to the river. His only chance.

The craft shuddered, and seemed to hang for a moment, then, as if in a sudden burst of will, it catapulted forward and down. But there was enough momentum to carry it over the water's edge.

David swung the door open and leaped.

He hit the water and plunged deep into its cool depths.

A hundred feet ahead, the helicopter struck the water and exploded.

*"Yassim Sivad is a murdering butcher!"* chanted the pickets. Over and over again as they marched in a circle.

The motorcade arrived; the Arab dignitaries spilled out of the limousines, followed by Sivad's security men.

*"Yassim Sivad is a murdering butcher!"*

Sivad emerged from his car. He raised his arms to the crowd in greeting, as if the catcalls he received were sounds of welcome.

Sivad, surrounded by his bodyguards and the dignitaries, walked slowly across the plaza toward the Perplax screen, smiling, waving to the TV cameras.

*"Yassim Sivad is a murdering butcher!"*

Sivad took his place on the podium behind the Perplax; the bodyguards tensely watching the crowds; the police on the alert.

"My friends," began Sivad. "In a few moments I will have the honor to address the General Assembly of the United Nations and the people of the West. Here in this great city of New York, I stand before you, pleading that you hear the anguished cries of the Palestinians banished from their homeland."

*"Yassim Sivad is a murdering butcher!"*

"Hear this, my friends . . ."

*The pigeons circled high above the plaza.*

". . . It is you who must end this evil partnership between your government and the gangsters of Tel Aviv."

*Now they began the descent. Swooping.*

A TV crewman looked up and observed to his buddy, "How about that! Doves of peace."

*The pigeons, the tiny containers dangling from the chains around their necks, continued their downward plunge.*

*"Yassim Sivad is a murdering butcher!"*

Sivad looked up at the sound of the wings beating the still air. An omen? He smiled.

"Observe!" He extended his arms upward. "I welcome you!"

*They came down in formation like guided planes; as they'd been doing these many months; to swoop and take off again.*

*The plastique screen was clear. Shadowless. Stationed exactly at the birds' take-off point. Only they'd never take off again. Training completed.*

*Sivad ducked reflexively just before the pigeons crashed into the clear* Perplax.

He did not see:

*The blinding flash!*

He did not hear:

*The doomsday crack!*

*Louder than thunder!*

*A tremendous fireball!*

*A continuous roar as the entire facade of the U.N. Building fell away!*

*Thick smoke billowed upward like an atomic mushroom!*

*In slow-motion cadence the building began to crumble!*

Inside the General Assembly Hall, the walls were gone; the roof shorn away. The gallery, filled to capacity, broke apart. The roar drowned out the horrified cries. Dust billowed and obscured the slaughter.

Outside, the deafening roar continued while thick smoke mercifully blotted out the carnage.

Gradually, the terrible sound subsided and the smoke began to drift away. Then there was stillness.

The stillness of death.

More terrifying than the roar.

Stark devastation remained.

# PART TWO

# 19

*Washington, D.C.*
*Friday Evening*

"Ladies and gentlemen, the president of the United States."

The president entered the Oval Office and took his seat at his desk. He turned his somber gaze on the lens of the TV camera that had the red light, then gave his attention to the teleprompter that showed him the words he'd written before the fact.

*"My fellow Americans . . . this morning, men's souls were seared by the butchery which had taken place at the site of the United Nations.*

*"Bloated with madness and blinded by a paranoiac craving for vengeance, a foreign government struck a terrible, bloody blow against innocent people of all nations . . ."*

145

He shifted his gaze into the lens of the camera: "*All nations except one.*"

He paused. His voice trembled.

"*I accuse the state of Israel and its agents in America of perpetrating this horrendous crime! And I have the evidence to prove it!*"

The signal.

Wagner's cells went into action.

The major cities of the world became scenes of rampage and riot. Destruction with bombs and fire. Smashed store windows. Lootings and beatings and rape.

The police made no move to intercede.

And the cry went up: "Jew! Jew! Jew!"

And the state of Israel waited for the expected invasion.

*Waited with her arsenal of atomic bombs.*


## Night

On the island of Guam, General Marley met with leaders of the Soviet Union, China and Japan. Prearranged. In camera.

The agenda: Spheres of influence. As blueprinted by Julius Lipman.

As the planet seethed.

David reached his building, bloody and exhausted. He had spent most of the day in a hospital ward, having been picked up as one of the victims of the disaster at the U.N. They found him wandering, dazed and disoriented.

He had remained confined throughout the day, his wounds tended to. Night found him out on the street.

It was all clear to him now. Why Wagner and

company wanted him alive. The conspiracy: to blame him for the destruction, acting as agent for Israel.

But how would they prove the lie?

He had tried calling the penthouse; to tell Lippy he was safe. No answer. Someone had to be there. Were they waiting for him? To place him under arrest?

Should he run?

It would be evidence of guilt. His and Israel's.

The streets were in full riot when he left the hospital. Madness. Decimation rampant. Stores and homes laid to waste. Destruction. Chaos. Carnage en toto.

He managed to find a cab, got in and directed the driver to the Thirty-eighth Street Synagogue.

The driver jumped out and jerked open the rear door. He called David a "fuckin' Jew" and pulled him out.

He never saw David's hands fly; neither did he feel the pain at the shredding of his face. Just a sharp, sudden burning, short-lived. Then blackness. He lay in the gutter to be trampled by the rioters.

David drove the cab to the synagogue. It was no more. Smoking ruins.

In Harlem he went in search of King.

He was told that King had been garrotted for being a Jew-lover.

David wept and beat his breast and cried out to God in despair, demanding to know why he had been chosen as the instrument of death.

He did not expect an answer.

He pushed his way through the revolving door of his building and found the lobby deserted. No guards. No people. No hope.

He got into the elevator and sent it up.

He leaned weakly against its walls, his eyes closed, his face a reflection of his pain. The awful sequence of events pounded his mind; flooded it with guilt because he could have stopped it.

*Sh'ma Yisrael, Adonai Elohaynu, Adonai Ehad.*

He staggered out of the elevator and stumbled into the sitting room.

They were there as he suspected they would be.

Carl Fredericks and four FBI agents.

They stood there—impassive; made no move toward him.

Lipman was with them. "I've called the lawyers, David," he said soberly. "You'll be free in a couple of hours."

"Don't bank on it, Lippy," said David. "We don't have a chance." He turned to Fredericks. "What's the charge, Fredericks?"

"Murder in the first degree," replied Fredericks. "Conspiracy to commit murder. Treason."

David smiled. His hand flew out in a swift arc. It never reached its target. The gun butt behind his ear put him to sleep.

# 20

## Washington, D.C.
## Dawn

The president was unhappy. He knew that Martin
Simon, the attorney general, would make a scene. The
president didn't like scenes. They made him uncom-
fortable. But he had Secretary of State Brandon with
him. And William Stoll, his chief of staff. That helped
to ease the discomfort. Brandon always knew what
to do. And Stoll was extremely capable. They could
handle Martin Simon.

He glanced at his watch and scowled. Where the
hell was he?

The way Martin Simon strode into the Oval Office
made the president wince. Simon was a small man but
he burned with an energy that had always made the
president uneasy.

"Goddamn it, Charlie," shouted Simon, "the police for some fucking reason wouldn't act, and the governors didn't call out the National Guard, and you refused to have the army stop all the shit that went on. What the hell was on your mind?"

"Take it easy, Martin," said the president, placatingly.

"Take it easy my ass! The way you fired up the people with your outrageous speech was nothing less than criminal. It'll be impossible for Ring to get a fair trial."

Brandon donned a benign look. "Let us worry about that, Martin."

"Bullshit!" Martin was not to be mollified. "It's *my* worry. I have to try this man, and from all the evidence handed me, the case is open and shut. But where the hell am I going to get an impartial jury?"

"You have a point," said Brandon in his best assumed judicious manner. A hint of his schoolboy pout played at the edges of his mouth.

Stoll sat clipping his nails. He was a man of medium build with curly dark hair, a small mustache and a confident manner.

"He's obviously guilty, Martin," said the president. "In view of the nature and scope of this horrendous crime, why can't we suspend trial by jury?"

"Would you also suspend the Supreme Court?" said Martin, sarcastically. "The Constitution?"

"If it became necessary."

"Holy Christ!"

"What Charlie means," interposed Brandon, "is that in certain emergencies the rights of the people may have to be held in abeyance. Temporarily, of course."

Simon felt a gnawing fear. "What the hell are you talking about?"

"Martial law."

"What?"

"Didn't you just tell me that I should have called out the army?" The president gave him an ingenuous look.

"Sure," said Martin thinly. "To stop the rioting. Not to start a revolution."

"Revolution is an ugly word, Martin," said the president, wincing.

"We're having Ring transferred to Washington," said Brandon. "For his own protection. He's got to be brought to trial swiftly. And upon being found guilty you are to demand that he be executed by a firing squad." Then he added: "In full view of the television cameras."

"A circus!"

"Correct."

"And you've already convicted him before trial."

"Just a matter of going through the motions."

"You don't know what you're talking about! Ring will have the most brilliant legal minds in the country defending him."

"Open and shut, Martin."

"But innocent until proven guilty."

"Shit on that!" cried the president, his face contorted with hatred.

The attorney general looked from one to the other narrowly. "Hey—what's going on?"

"Relax, Martin," said Brandon. He might have been warding off the bullies in the schoolyard.

"Balls! What are you guys up to? I swore to uphold the Constitution. So did you, Charlie. And you, too, Leonard. Now you're bent on burying it."

"Emergency, Martin," explained the president, his voice now under control. "The people want satisfaction. When that tape outlining the conspiracy is played at the trial and carried around the world, we've got to be ready to maintain order. Law and order. That's what this country is all about, Martin. I don't have to tell *you*. You're the law man. And as commander-in-chief of the armed forces I'm in charge of the order department." He leaned back in his chair, closed his eyes and made a tent with his fingers. "Also, we must be prepared to try the state of Israel in the world council. For conspiracy and mass murder."

*Sharp and clear*, thought Martin. *A takeover! Not by the communists, but by the far right. God help us.*

He calmed himself somewhat. He wanted to see if he could button down their perfidy. "Supposing," he said, "that the defense proves that the tape is a phony."

The president cast a quick look at Brandon.

"It's authentic," said Brandon.

"Suppose."

"We'll have our experts testify to its authenticity."

"You mean they've already examined the tape?"

"Not yet."

"Suppose *they* say the tape is a phony."

"They won't."

"Suppose."

"They won't."

"How do you know?"

"Because they're *our* experts."

Pause. "Is it a phony?"

"The director of the FBI will testify that he recorded it word for word. As it came through the bug. By the way, did I tell you I've named Carl Fredericks as the new FBI director?"

"Thanks for the information," Simon said dryly. "But you didn't answer my question."

152

"The tape is authentic."

"I think you're a frigging liar." He turned to the president. "You know something, Charlie? David Ring is not one of your schnooks. He's a power. Not only that, he has the saintly reputation of being against the forces of Evil. If it is proved that all the evidence presented by us is one big frame-up, your life won't be worth a plugged nickel." He got up from his chair. "You'll get my letter of resignation within the hour." And he stormed out of the room.

The president turned a pained face to Brandon. "Jesus, Leonard—"

"Don't worry, Charlie," said Brandon. "Just don't worry."

The chief of staff finally spoke. "There's nothing to worry about, Charlie," he said. "Your place in history is assured."

The president's eyes flicked around the room, and under his breath he said, "Yeah."

# *21*

A hearing was held in the federal court, southern district, county of New York on defendant's motion for the posting of bail.

Denied.

Habeas corpus.

Denied.

*Motion by prosecutor in the case of the United States versus David Ring for the transfer of the hereinabove titled matter to the District of Columbia.*

Granted.

Fredericks, in the company of four FBI agents, marched into a detention cell in the Federal Building, handcuffed David, and together marched out to a waiting limousine.

They drove to a corner of the airfield at Kennedy where a 707 was parked, its engines warming.

Big plane for such a short run.

The four FBI agents escorted David up the portable stairway into the interior.

The door was locked shut and the stair was pulled away.

Fredericks stood alongside the limousine; watched the plane taxi to its assigned position and waited for it to become airborne.

He then entered the limousine and gave Brandon's number to the telephone operator.

"He's on his way," he told Brandon. "Advise the president as planned."

In the cockpit of the 707 the pilot guided the plane to its cruising altitude. The flight engineer and the navigator studied their charts. The copilot checked the instruments.

*They spoke to each other in Arabic.*

*They expected to reach Damascus in ten hours.*

The president was addressing the American people on television.

Righteously indignant.

"The act of piracy and kidnapping that occurred this afternoon was not only an affront to the people of the United States of America, but was also an ignominious slap in the face of your president.

"To permit this outrage to go unchallenged would be, in the eyes of the world, a confession of our sterility and would brand your president a coward.

"*I am not a coward!* Therefore, my fellow Americans, with the unanimous approval of my cabinet, the members of our Security Council, the leaders of Congress, I have ordered our armed forces on standby alert and have issued an ultimatum to the government of Syria that if David Ring is not returned to us within twenty-four hours, our missiles will become operative."

Millah Dasat, the president of Syria, replied on television.

"As president of my country, I hereby state unequivocally, that we have no quarrel with America.

"A monstrous crime has been committed against the Arab people for which we do not seek revenge but justice."

Lipman sat in David's study watching the telecast, sucking on a cold pipe.

"A conviction of David Ring procured in the American courts would have to be overturned since an impartial jury could not be impaneled, and thus David Ring would go free."

Secretary of State Brandon and the president watched the speech from the Oval Office.

"Here in Damascus, the accused will be tried before a panel of seven judges. All heads of state will be invited to act as observers. Television cameras will beam the event to the four corners of the globe.

"I offer the president of the United States justice. If he still desires to destroy my country . . . so be it."

Brandon turned off the set. "Pretty good speech."

The president wasn't so sure. "You think so?" He frowned.

"Makes sense."

"What do you mean?"

"It'll be more effective if he's tried in Syria than here. Justice will be swifter."

"I have a feeling," said the president, eyeing him narrowly, "that you arranged for the hijack."

Brandon smiled crookedly. "How else could you have made such a great speech to inflame the country?" the little fat man said.

"What do I do about the ultimatum?"

"Make another speech. A retraction in the cause of justice. Makes you look good."

"Yes." The president nodded thoughtfully. "Good idea. I like that."

Brandon started for the door. "I'm on my way. I'll keep in touch."

"Where are you going?"

"Damascus." He grinned. "Somebody's got to deliver the evidence."

Brandon left. The president took a sheet of paper and began to write.

*My fellow Americans . . .*

# 22

## Damascus, Syria

The lone passenger got out of the taxi in front of Mezza Prison.

He was a tall, slender Syrian; well dressed, small mustache, trim beard. Strikingly handsome. His voice had a gentle sound when he thanked the driver.

With a firm step he moved toward the entrance.

David lay on a cot in the small cell, his hands interlocked behind his head, his mind stewing over the recent happenings.

Was there still time?

Who was left to help? Harry, Jonathan, Al—all gone.

Could Lippy and Myrna do it?

Lippy had to be led; Myrna was a hope.

He was not concerned for himself. But for America. For Israel. For all the Jews in the world. For all the people.

*Impossible.*

*It couldn't happen.*

*But it was happening.*

He heard the approaching footsteps echoing along the corridor.

A visitor?

No one ever came to see him. Except the guards who brought him his meals. Too early for that.

His was the only cell on the floor. He was special. They had told him it was for his own protection. Here he was safe. No other prisoners near to do him harm.

He had smiled when they told him that. How could they know the strength in his hands?

He heard the door unlock, then saw the guard admit the visitor. He got up slowly, eyeing the man curiously.

"Please sit," said the man. Then he added, "How have they been treating you?" He sat beside David.

"Much too well," said David. "Considering the horrible crime I'm accused of."

"You think you're being fattened up for the slaughter." It was a statement.

"I couldn't have said it better. . . . Who are you?"

"I have been granted permission to represent you at the trial."

"Why would you want to do that?"

"I believe you're innocent."

"Really?" said David dubiously.

"Knowing you as I do—by reputation, of course—you could not have been responsible for the U.N. slaughter."

"Thanks. But you'll have your hands full trying to convince the world of that."

"All we have to do is satisfy four of the seven judges."

"Simple as that."

"Far from it. However, our attorney general must convince the majority of the court of your guilt."

"Now *that* should be real simple."

"Not quite. We have a presumption of innocence until guilt is proved."

"Even when it involves a Jew?"

"We adhere to the principles of equality under the law."

"Bullshit."

"Right." He grinned. "How's Myrna?"

David tossed him a startled look. What did he know about Myrna?

"And Lippy . . . and Harry, and Jonathan, and Al?"

"Who the hell are you?" David got to his feet.

"You mean I've changed that much?" The man stood up and stroked his beard. "The beard, perhaps."

David stared at him, jogging his memory.

"I'd recognize you anywhere," continued Hafez. "Even after thirty years . . . when we were eight years old."

A long pause. "Hafez!"

"Hi, David," said Hafez softly.

Tears came to David's eyes. His voice broke. "Hafez . . ."

They embraced. It was a long while before David could trust his voice. Then he said: "You son of a bitch!" And they embraced again.

And they came around to the present.

"How did you ever get into this mess?" asked Hafez.

David sighed. "You won't believe who's involved.

Our secretary of state, a senator, a retired four-star general, that neo-Nazi, Klaus Wagner, the FBI and most likely the president of the United States. We're on the verge of a Nazi takeover, Hafez. It's the most fantastic conspiracy ever committed against the people of the world!"

"I have an appointment with our attorney general," said Hafez, "to see what evidence they have on you. We'll plan our defense accordingly."

"Right. But keep in mind the theory of conspiracy."

"It might be difficult to prove, David."

"Of course. But we've got a lot of contacts in Washington. Anything you need, call Lippy."

*Call Lippy.*

They sat on the cot and filled in the thirty years.

## Lake George, N.Y.

In her motel room, Myrna was on the phone to Lipman. "I don't know what I'm looking for, Lippy. I've gone over every inch of those grounds and came up empty. . . . What's the news on David?"

He told her about Hafez handling David's defense. And: "I've got to fly to Washington and see the Israeli ambassador. He's got a tape of a conversation with Major Benn Yussid that could help David . . . keep looking Myrna, let me know the minute you find anything."

Myrna replied, "We're going out again this afternoon. The Lake George police department started to give us trouble but we showed them some green and they backed off. . . . When you talk to Hafez tell him we love him."

She hung up and wept.

# Washington, D.C.

The Israeli ambassador had been packing and shredding papers. Diplomatic relations between the United States and Israel were broken. He and Lipman stood before an open wall safe. "I kept it here," the ambassador said. "They didn't touch anything else."

"Didn't you make a copy?" asked Lipman.

"Of course not. Who would have thought anybody would want it?"

"That tape, Mr. Ambassador," said Lipman, "was an important piece of evidence for David's defense."

"My God! How did they know it existed? . . . Who are they?"

"Could be anyone. Even a member of your own staff."

"Nonsense."

Lipman checked his watch. "I'd better be getting back. Let's hope Myrna is able to come up with something. Shalom."

"Shalom," murmured the ambassador.

# Damascus, Syria

David stood in front of the barred window, letting the sunlight warm his face. He turned expectantly when the guard unlocked the door to admit Hafez.

"We struck out, David," said Hafez. "The ambassador's safe was broke into. The tape is gone."

"Naturally," said David, his tone bitter. "They knew it existed; they knew it could clear me. It had to be destroyed. What did Lippy have to say?"

"He's frustrated. We're in trouble, David."

163

"There's still one last hope. I told you about Anna Thornton and her dying words. She got as far as saying the words: '*Lake George—look . . .*'" He took a deep breath. "Myrna's looking. God knows for what. But whatever it is, she'll find it." But his despair showed. "Before I face a firing squad, Hafez, there's something I've got to do. Will you help me?"

"Anything, David. With my life!"

# 23

Hafez made several purchases. Spools of thin piano wire. A wire cutter. A straight razor. Shaving material. A bottle of spirit gum. A roll of adhesive tape. A false black beard and mustache. Gelatin capsules.

In his apartment, Hafez shaved his beard and mustache, washed and dried his face, then applied the spirit gum and pressed the false beard and mustache firmly in place.

He then filled the empty capsules with the viscous spirit gum.

He changed into a dark suit and examined his reflection from all angles. He gave the beard a final pat and turned away satisfied.

The taxi dropped him at the prison gate. Before entering he concealed the capsules in his beard.

Inside, he underwent the usual search. The guards found nothing.

He was escorted to David's cell.

They waited until the sound of the guard's footsteps faded to stillness.

Then they worked swiftly, wasting no time with words.

First the exchange of clothes; finally the beard and mustache went into place, using the spirit gum from the capsules. The transformation from David to Hafez was startling. Hafez assuming David's identity might not pass a close inspection. But why, in his cell, should he be inspected closely?

In perfect Arabic, David directed the taxi driver to Hafez' apartment. It was early evening.

He found an attaché case containing the razor, the wire and wire cutter, the roll of adhesive tape . . . and a small Beretta. . . .

He hurried out to the taxi and was taken to the Hotel Metropole.

David crossed the lobby to the desk and greeted the clerk in Arabic.

The clerk looked up and smiled. "Good evening. May I help you?"

"If you will. I am the government information director and I have important messages for our visitors from America. Could you direct me to the rooms of . . ." He took a note from his pocket and read: ". . . Klaus Wagner, Carl Fredericks, General Marley, Senator Franklyn, Secretary Brandon and Reverend Carson."

"Mr. Wagner and Mr. Fredericks went out a short while ago," said the clerk, bowing with deference. "General Marley is entertaining the others in his suite." He reached for the phone. "I will be happy to call."

David stayed his hand. "That won't be necessary. I wish to surprise them. I have a message from the president."

"Of course . . . General Marley is in suite DD on the fourth floor."

"Thank you kindly."

"You are welcome."

The clerk, wearing a proud expression, watched David leave for the elevator.

David stepped out onto the fourth floor corridor; paused for a moment to get his bearings.

The elevator operator noticed his indecision. "May I help you, sir?"

"I'm looking for suite DD."

"Fourth door on your right, sir."

"Thank you." He proceeded along the corridor until he came to it. He quickly removed the beard and mustache, and placed it in the attaché case for future use.

Marley was refilling the champagne glasses held by Brandon, Carson and Franklyn.

"In less than a week, gentlemen," the lanky ex-general was telling them, "the world will witness the slickest takeover of a country since Hitler's Third Reich."

"Hear! Hear!" crowed Carson, struggling to overcome the curvature of his spine to stand erect.

"How strong are we in Canada?" Franklyn wanted to know, his stentorian voice rumbling. "Their riots hadn't been as organized as we'd have liked."

"We've cut out their dead wood," said Brandon. "They'll fall into line. Just as Mexico has." The fat man raised his glass. "Drink hearty and stop worrying."

The door buzzer sounded.

"That must be Klaus and Carl," said Marley.

He put down the bottle and the glass and crossed to the foyer and opened the door.

"May I come in?" said David, smiling.

"*My God!*" Marley's voice was a hoarse rasp. The horror in it was unmistakable.

*How was it possible? It couldn't be!*

Brandon's voice was heard. "Who is it, Alex?"

What could Marley say? Especially when David waved the Beretta and whispered: "Don't tell him. Let's surprise him."

David closed the door behind him and pushed Marley ahead of him into the room.

The others saw him. They were stunned. Unable to move. Paralyzed with shock and fear.

"Sit down, Marley." David shoved him into a chair.

David felt sick at the sight of them. If only he could drain their blood drop by drop; suffer them with boils and running sores; slow spreading cancers not strong enough to kill but enough to possess them with permanent pain for which there was no analgesic.

He saw the champagne. "I don't usually drink with pigs," said David, absorbing with pleasure the terror in their faces. "But tonight is an exceptional night."

He filled their glasses and one for himself. "To justice," he said. "May her blindfold be removed just this once so that she may see the scum she has to deal with . . . *L'chaim!* . . . That means, 'to life'— but not yours."

David drained his glass. The others sat motionless. Except Marley.

"You don't scare me, Ring," he sneered. He smashed the glass to the floor. "If you're gonna shoot,

168

go ahead. I've been a soldier too long to be afraid of death."

David's face broke into a wide grin. He moved closer to him. "Well, now, Herr General. If a bullet doesn't scare you, what does? Obviously, murdering thousands of innocent people at the U.N. didn't affect you. Perhaps even gave you pleasure. Therefore, you and death are . . . like pals, right? If you're not afraid to die, what could possibly frighten you?" He wrinkled his brow in mock thought. "I wonder if . . . I've got it! How about this?"

With a lightning move, David's hand streaked out and cut down alongside of Marley's head, *cleanly slicing off his ear*.

Marley let out a scream of terror and pain. At the same moment David's hand grabbed Marley's shirt-front and tore off a handful of cloth. He pressed it against the side of the general's head to stanch the blood.

Marley held the cloth in place.

"Now," David went on, "if that doesn't scare you, I might try your nose. Would you like me to try?"

Marley glowered but he shook his head.

"Now would you like to drink my toast?"

He nodded.

"Good." David picked up the glass from the floor, filled it and handed it to Marley. "Be careful. Don't drip blood in it. Unless you like sparkling burgundy. All right, everybody, drink up."

Almost simultaneously they drained their glasses. They stood, silenced, gripped by fear.

David's manner turned from flip to loathing. "You miserable, murdering bastards!"

He removed the spool of piano wire from the attaché case and tossed it to Carson. "Tie their wrists behind their backs, then extend the wire to their ankles. On the bare flesh. If they struggle, hopefully they might sever an artery."

"Now look here—" began Brandon.

"One more word out of you," said David between his teeth, "and I'll cut your tongue out. . . . go to work, Carson."

While Carson began working on Brandon and Franklyn, David—with a second spool of wire—tied the general's wrists positioned in such a manner that the cloth at his ear was held in place.

He ran the wire from the general's wrists around his neck and to his ankles. Using the cutter, he snipped the wire; then turned to examine Carson's work. "Very good. Now to take care of you."

After binding Carson in the same manner he pushed them roughly onto the sofa.

"Hop over here, general, and join your friends. . . . Careful, I wouldn't want you to be decapitated."

David wired the four of them together, encircling their necks to limit movement. This done, he sealed their mouths with adhesive tape. Finished, he stepped back to view his work.

"Not bad," he said. "Not bad at all."

He refilled his champagne glass, drained it, and was about to pour another when the door buzzer sounded.

He placed the bottle down and crossed to the foyer; opened the door to face Wagner and Fredericks.

The skin on Wagner's forehead was raw and scarred. It was obvious that Doctor Gagliano hadn't done a creditable plastic job to cover the engraved swastika that marred the handsome Aryan features.

"Come in," greeted David. "Come in. There's work to be done." He beckoned with his gun.

Dazed, they entered the room, speechless, horror-struck.

There they were—six psychopathic criminals; fanatical leaders, indiscriminate murderers, conspirators.

David could have ended their lives.

There.

In that room.

But it was not his choice to make.

Instead, David bound the two new arrivals in wire and joined them with the others, and with his straight razor struck the mark of Cain on all their foreheads.

Swastikas.

The phone rang.

David flashed a curious look at them. For whom? From whom?

He moved toward it, slowly, wondering whether he should answer it.

He placed his hand on the instrument; the ringing shrill and insistent, like a beating heart.

David picked it up.

"Hello . . . ?"

The switchboard operator said, "There is an overseas call for you, general. Washington, D.C. Will you take it?"

Pause. "Yes."

"One moment, please."

A moment. Then another. And another.

An eternity.

"Hold on, please."

Hold . . . hold . . . hold . . .

"Hello . . ."

Static.

"Hello . . . hello. . . ?"

"Yes . . . ?"

"General?"

"Yes . . ." said David weakly.

"I can't hear you."

"I can barely hear you. Who is this?"

"Your voice sounds strange."

"It's the static. Who is this?"

*"Lipman here, general. Julius."*

A shudder shook David's frame. The room swam; he grabbed the table for support.

"General?"

Pause. Then: "Yes?" He glanced at the bound conspirators. They must not know who was calling.

"I'm in the Oval Office with the president," said Lipman. "He wants you to leave Damascus immediately after the trial. You are to take command as soon as his declaration of martial law is issued."

David's mind spun in a whirlpool of bewilderment.

Words spilled out of the receiver; words of takeover—mass arrests—genocide.

*Lippy! Lippy! Lippy!*

*Oh, God! What are you doing to me?*

Dazed, he cradled the phone, and with the razor cut the cord, then, with faltering steps he left the room, pausing to place the DO NOT DISTURB sign on the doorknob.

# 24

"Operator—" David jiggled the riser on the telephone in Hafez' apartment. "Operator—"

She answered.

"This is Hafez Ameer. I wish to place a call to New York City—to a Myrna Lu. Area code 212-476-2552. If she does not answer, keep trying every half hour. I will be standing by. Thank you."

He could not remember how he had managed to reach Hafez' apartment. He'd moved as if in a hypnotic state. Walking miles. The horror of Lipman's betrayal had left him numb with despair.

He hung up the phone and flung himself into a chair, sobbing in anguish. Then, completely spent, he slept.

At the first light, he stirred, then woke with a start. His mind cleared. He remembered.

Myrna!

Had he slept through the ringing of the phone?

"Operator . . . I had placed a call to New York City. Were you able to get through? . . . I see. Keep trying."

He bathed, applied the beard and mustache, selected a fresh suit and left for the prison.

Hafez lay on a cot, his back to the barred door. He heard it being unlocked; he did not stir. Even when David entered. It was only when the guard's footsteps could no longer be heard that he leaped from the cot.

"Hurry," said David, starting to undress.

"How did it go?"

"Without a hitch."

"You shouldn't have come back."

"And leave you here?" He tossed him a warm smile. "You know what they'd do to you?"

"Your life is more worthy than mine."

"That's not true . . . but I thank you, my good friend."

They made the rest of the change of clothing in silence. Then David said, "Hafez, who do you think is the true leader of the world Nazi movement?"

Hafez eyed him curiously. "Not Klaus Wagner?"

David shook his head. "You'll be shocked."

Hafez waited.

"Lippy," said David.

"What?" Stunned.

David filled him in. "After the trial, martial law will be declared in the States. There'll be a complete takeover by the military. I couldn't get through to Myrna. You've got to warn her. It's up to her now, Hafez. You and Myrna."

They embraced. Hafez signaled the prison guard and he was let out.

David sank onto the cot and held his head in his hands.

## *Washington, D.C.*
## *The Oval Office*

"The trial will begin in exactly forty-eight hours," said Lipman on the phone to the head of Security.

The president behind his desk looked up from his writing.

"I want every cell leader on the alert," continued Lipman. "General Marley will take command and give the signal for the mass arrests. You will not be contacted again until this first episode is completed."

He listened and then became angry. "No, damn it! The chief justice and Judge Harmon are to be spared. What the hell's the matter with you! The seven others are to be interned. Understand?"

He demanded a recap.

The sweep was to include the secretary of defense and the chief of the NATO forces. Fortunately, Vice-President Barton had been one of the victims of the U.N. explosion.

"What do we do about the commander at Andrews?" Security wanted to know.

"For the time being General Turley is needed," Lipman told him. "Let's keep an eye on him. If he doesn't fall in line we'll replace him. . . . Anything else?"

Lipman was satisfied.

General Turley, commander of Andrews Air Force Base, sat in a darkened room of his cottage at the base, and brooded.

A quart bottle of bourbon on an end table beside his chair, nearly empty.

Cigarette butts in an ashtray. Overflowing.
An empty bottle on the floor.
His chin dropped to his chest.
His mind a jumble of terrible thoughts.
*It won't be long now before . . .*
*Too late to get out . . .*
*Gotta pay the piper . . .*
*Mephisto come to claim the soul of General*
*Faust . . .*
Painful laughter.
Sobs even more painful.
They made him chief of the base. They made him
a general. They made him a hangman.
Guilt racked his brain, tore at his spirit.
He drained the bottle and tossed the empty across
the room. He staggered to his feet, stood swaying for
a moment, then weaved his way to the bedroom and
collapsed on the bed in a stupor.

# 25

## Lake George, N.Y.

The search went on.

The burned-out ruins of the mansion were combed and recombed.

For what?

Myrna carefully examined the fireplace and chimney, the only thing left intact. That and the cement foundation. She used a poker to stir the ashes of the firebrick floor while the men used rakes and shovels and metal detectors in and around the foundation.

It all had been done before, over and over again. Something had to be there. Something.

She noted the state trooper standing at a distance watching the operation. She wondered about him.

The poker struck metal.

Myrna called out.

One of the men came running and swept the fire-place clean of ashes.

There it was. A metal plate implanted in the fire-brick floor. How was it she'd missed it before?

It covered a deep opening where the ashes were disposed of after they had grown cold.

It was three-quarters full.

The state trooper moved closer.

The man worked swiftly. Myrna watched, scarcely breathing. Was it there? The thing? Whatever?

Empty.

Her helper broke through the floor and the sides with a sledge. The bricks fell away revealing nothing.

Myrna shivered.

She stood by the lake on the boat dock not seeing nor hearing, nor feeling. Numb.

"I'm sorry, David." She owed him so much. She had been a drug addict in limbo. Until he breathed life into her. And she became whole.

A bird fluttered across a clump of cedars. A crow called; another answered. Across the lake the sun began sinking behind the pines.

She rowed the small boat out into the still water. Slowly, aimlessly, sightlessly.

She paused and looked about her. Surprised. She couldn't remember getting into the boat.

She dropped her oars and covered her face with her hands and wept bitterly. Then, in a fit of anger she pounded the sides of her head with her fists and turned her wet face to the sky. "*Why him?*"

Then she asked: "Why the innocent thousands at the U.N.? Why the vermin like Klaus Wagner and company?"

Now her wrath burning: "You know something, dear God?" She paused to make sure He was listening. "*I don't believe you exist! You're a figment—the creation of our self-pity. We built you to suit our needs. But how is it Klaus Wagner's God is stronger than David Ring's?"*

A fish jumped. The fly wasn't quick enough.

She laughed. "If you don't exist why am I talking to you? I guess you're there, all right. But you like to pick and choose, right? The games gods play! What do you say when you're through playing? Do you say, 'So long, sucker'? Okay. I heard you loud and clear."

It was when she picked up the oars to insert them into the oarlocks that it happened. The flat side of one of the oars flipped open the hinged lid of the fish well in the center of the boat.

Her nose wrinkled at the stench exuding from it. She leaned forward and saw the decayed fish floating in the water.

A wave of nausea came over her and she quickly shut the lid.

*There was something else in there. Something at the bottom. She had seen it in the split second it had taken the cover to drop.*

She no longer noticed the foul odor as she reached into the fish well. Only a tightening in her chest and the blood pounding in her ears.

*It was a waterproof pouch containing a cassette.* Myrna's lower lip trembled. "Please—God."

# 26

The state trooper had her in his glasses.

No hurry.

He'd wait until she left the grounds.

Myrna sped along the highway, her heart still pounding. What would the tape reveal? How important was it?

It had to be something big. Didn't Anna Thornton try to tell David? With her dying breath?

She reached out to touch her handbag that lay beside her. As if to caress the cassette inside.

*What hand had moved the oar to push up the lid of the fish well?*

"Forgive me, dear God," she murmured.

The sound of the siren in the distance caused her

to look into the rearview mirror. She saw the red light flashing. The sound and the light were coming up fast.

Her eyes dropped to the speedometer. The needle touched 75.

"Damn."

She pulled off the road and waited for the trooper to come to her.

He was very polite. He wasted no time in preliminaries. "May I see your license, ma'am?"

Myrna opened her bag, eyeing him narrowly. The trooper who was watching the search? She was sure of it. Had he been tailing her?

Careful.

He examined the license for a moment then said, "Will you step out of the car, please?"

"Why?"

"Please."

She took her handbag with her.

He reached for it.

*Mistake.*

Myrna had him on the ground. Her elbow pressed into his trachea until he lost consciousness. He'd have trouble speaking for a while.

She dragged him into the shrubbery and disposed of his gun.

No car passed.

She walked to the trooper's car and examined the interior.

Nothing. No police radio. No identification. It was as she suspected. That trooper was a phony.

She drove his car off the road, then fixed it so that it couldn't be driven.

She returned to the unconscious imposter and fixed it so he couldn't get far when he recovered.

She left him stark naked.

A sign across the front window of the store on Main Street read: ACKERMANN'S TV AND RECORDING SERVICE. Myrna remembered passing the store on the way to the burned-out mansion from the motel. She hoped Mr. Ackermann had a tape deck in stock.

Henry Ackermann had many tape decks in stock. All sorts of recording equipment and TV parts. And electronic devices. *When Myrna entered he was in the back room assembling and packing components for plastic explosives.*

*Henry Ackermann was the local Nazi cell leader.*

He knew about Myrna's search; he'd watched the operation several times. Didn't know what they were looking for. He had been alerted that Myrna was in charge. Now she was in his store.

*Why did she need a tape player?*

The moment she left he called the motel.

Ralph Hobson, manager of the Lake George Motel, let himself into Myrna's room to check on the concealed listening devices.

They were in place.

He unlocked the door to the adjoining room to test the tape recorder.

Voice-activated and in working order.

He returned to the front desk. Curious.

With a trembling hand Myrna unlocked the door to her room, praying silently as she did so. If the cassette was *something*, how much time did she have to save David? If it was *something* would *they* who held him believe?

She plugged in the tape deck, inserted the cassette and pressed the start button. The tape spun slowly.

Surface noise. Nothing . . . nothing . . .

Myrna stared at the narrow ribbon, its motion inexorable. Mesmerized, her mind pressed for *something*.

*A sudden jumble of voices.*

Indistinguishable.

Laughter . . . words . . . *"hate is more"* . . . *"cannot"* . . . *"cheers"* . . . *"it"* . . . *"I"* . . . *"don't"* . . . *"you"* . . . laughter . . .

Then a voice above all the others: *"He's here!"*

Silence, except for the scraping of chairs.

The voice of Carl Fredericks: *"Gentlemen—Anna —may I present Klaus Wagner!"*

*Applause.*

FREDERICKS: *Klaus, in this room you see the group that represents the supreme power, the authority, the control of the Nazi movement in America.*

WAGNER: Es freud mich sehr.

FREDERICKS: *. . . Reverend Carson . . .*

CARSON: *An honor, Herr Wagner.*

WAGNER: *The honor is mine, reverend.*

FREDERICKS: *Senator Franklyn . . .*

FRANKLYN: *Welcome to our shores, Mr. Wagner.*

WAGNER: *Thank you, senator.*

FREDERICKS: *Secretary Brandon . . .*

BRANDON: *Indeed a pleasure.*

WAGNER: *King Achmed sends his best, Mr. Secretary.*

BRANDON: *Very kind.*

FREDERICKS: *General Marley . . .*

MARLEY: *We'll get some action now, eh Wagner?*

WAGNER: *Yes, we shall. With your help, of course.*

MARLEY: *You bet your ass.*

FREDERICKS: *And our charming hostess—Anna Thornton, the president's mistress.*

WAGNER: *The power behind the throne?*

ANNA: *That's a cliché, Herr Wagner.*

WAGNER: *How would you say it, madam?*

ANNA: *I'll let history fashion the words.*

WAGNER: *Touché. . . . Would you kindly all be seated. . . . Carl, if you don't mind, I would like to get started.*

FREDERICKS: *Please.*

WAGNER: *I will be brief. . . . I am pleased to inform you that the Arab bloc nations are in complete agreement with the aims of our cause and have placed at our disposal unlimited funds. At the outset, permit me to say that our prime objective is the elimination of David Ring and his organization. Not by the traditional means, but in such a manner, which, when accomplished, the act will be considered, in the eyes of the world, as heroic. As a result we will find ourselves in position of supreme power.*

BRANDON: *What did you have in mind, Herr Wagner?*

WAGNER: *First things first, Mr. Secretary. There is a mass of detail to be discussed and executed. What I would like to know is, does the basic idea please you?*

FRANKLYN: *The elimination of David Ring would please me no matter how achieved. That name sticks in my craw.*

MARLEY: *(a chuckle) Ring was instrumental in causing the defeat of the senator for reelection.*

FRANKLYN: *The bastard.*

MARLEY: *Come on, Klaus. You've got our appetite whetted. Let's hear the plan.*

ANNA: *Plot would be a better word. Right, Herr Wagner?*

WAGNER: *Precisely.*

BRANDON: *A plot can be exposed.*

WAGNER: *Not this one, Mr. Secretary. The secrecy of it is locked in this room. Not even our Arab friends are aware of it.*

CARSON: *Damn it, Klaus, what the hell is it?*

WAGNER: *Patience is bitter, yes reverend? But its fruit is sweet.*

CARSON: *Sorry.*

WAGNER: *In exactly seven days, Yassim Sivad, the leader of the Palestine Liberation Front, will address the General Assembly of the United Nations. You are well aware of this. Especially you, Mr. Secretary.*

BRANDON: *Yes. I had something to do with arranging it. Sub-rosa, of course.*

WAGNER: *Yes. . . . Present in the Assembly Hall will be seven hundred and fifty delegates representing the nations of the world, and thirteen hundred spectators. The representatives of the state of Israel will be conspicuous by their absence. Which fits the design. Yassim Sivad's presence, his words, his image, will be televised and carried by satellite to every part of the world. At which time . . .* (long pause) *the General Assembly Hall will be blown up.* (Gasps and murmurs from the group) *We will execute this deed in such a manner that overwhelming evidence will point to David Ring as the contractor on behalf of the Jewish state. The pending motion in the U.N. to expel Israel makes the timing perfect. What better motive is there for the U.N.'s destruction than revenge? . . . And for uncovering the evidence and exposing the crime our party will gain world prominence. The people will be ours. The rest of the world will fall in line. We have seven days. It shall be done.*

The tape ran out.

Myrna wept at the horror.

She lifted the phone and made a person-to-person call to Lipman.

He wasn't in. She left a message: "*Good news. Wait for me.*"

She called the airport and asked that her plane be readied.

She rewound the tape and placed the cassette in her handbag, leaving the tape deck. Its work was done.

Ralph Hobson left the front desk after Myrna checked out, then quickly made for the room that housed the recorder.

He rewound the tape, placed the phones to his ears and listened.

His eyes bulged and his mouth fell open.

His thoughts pounded in his skull.

**What!**

# 27

## New York City

Lipman watched the night traffic below from the penthouse garden overlooking the stately apartment houses bordering the East River Drive. He lived in one of them. Soon, he'd be moving to Washington. The White House.

The air was still; the smoke from his pipe drifted lazily.

Myrna's message . . . "Good news"? She must have found—whatever.

He rubbed the bowl of the pipe alongside his nose; the oil of his skin made the grain shine. His teeth clamped down hard on the stem and he puffed several times to get the glow going.

*Too late for good news, Myrna. Whatever it is, it'll*

*never leave the penthouse. . . . Nor will you.* Finito. Terminé.

He turned away from the parapet and walked slowly into David's study; the room he hated with a fury; full of reminders of David's successes, accolades, honors. And the one thing that tore at his insides: framed on the wall—the Nobel Prize in Economics. The honor he had strived for and which had been denied him.

No matter. It would be *his* name that would leave the greater mark on history. Not David's. Soon all will be brought to fruition and . . .

"Lippy!"

Myrna stood in the doorway, her eyes glistening, her face alive. "I found it!" She held the cassette aloft. "We're home free, Lippy!"

"My God, Myrna." He went to her. "What is it?"

She handed it to him. "Put it on the machine and find out. I'm calling Hafez." Lippy removed a tape deck from the desk drawer while Myrna placed the call.

"Did you make a copy?" asked Lippy.

"I didn't have a chance." Into the phone: "I'll hold, operator."

Lippy started the tape rolling. Myrna grinned, anticipating Lippy's reaction.

His expression was enigmatic.

The names.

The plan.

The plot.

The conspiracy.

He stared down at the moving tape, his teeth clenched on the pipe stem. The tobacco in the bowl charred. No glow.

He tapped it with his finger.

His hand went to his pocket and came out with

the gas lighted. He spun the wheel, and the flame leaped.

Myrna screamed and flung herself at him.

The lighter tumbled across the rug; Lippy picked himself up from the floor.

The tape continued telling its tale.

"I'm sorry, Lippy," said Myrna, her face pale. "Do you know how close you came to destroying the tape with that goddamn flame?"

"I didn't realize. It's incredible. It was as if I were hypnotized." He rubbed his wrist. "That small hand of yours packs a lot of power," he said ruefully.

The phone rang.

"Hafez!" She ran to the phone. "Hello? . . . Yes, operator." Long pause. Then: "Hafez! I found it! Tell David it's a tape of the Lake George meeting. It exposes the whole conspiracy. Names. Events. Schedules." She filled him in with the length and breadth of it. Suddenly, she halted and listened. Her expression turned to stone, her lips a thin line.

She replaced the receiver and slowly crossed back to Lipman; her attitude seemed the same as before the call, but her eyes had gone dead. The tape stopped rolling.

"Hafez was ecstatic," she said. "He suggested that we contact someone in government we can trust to get me to Damascus."

Lippy removed the cassette from the machine. "It might be a better idea if I went with you."

"No, Lippy. You have too much to do here. Besides, it'll be easier to clear one than two." She held out her hand for the cassette.

Lippy nodded. "You're right. Meanwhile, I'll make a copy of this." He started for the door, his back to her.

Myrna got the pistol out of the drawer. "Be careful," she said mockingly. "Don't pull a Rose Mary Woods."

He laughed and turned. He saw the pointed gun.

"You bastard," she said between her teeth. "You murdering son of a bitch."

Lipman gave her an impassive look. Silence, then: "How did Hafez find out?"

"Unimportant. Why did you do it?"

"Does it matter? It's over now, isn't it?"

"Not quite," she added bitterly. "David trusted you."

"That was his weakness."

"He loved you."

His face tightened. "David isn't capable of loving anyone."

"The tape, Lippy."

"You'll have to kill me."

"No. What I'll do is wound you very badly. When David comes back he'll decide what to do with you."

Lipman flung the cassette, staggering her. The gun fell from her hand.

He scrambled for it, but was no match for Myrna's speed. He lay on the floor, writhing in pain from a fractured clavicle.

Myrna stared down at him. "You almost got away with it." The pistol was pointed at his crotch. He screamed when the bullet hit.

She crossed to the phone and punched three digits. The hospital answered.

"Mr. Lipman is badly wounded," she said. "He's in the study. Send a stretcher and keep him under restraint until Mr. Ring returns."

Returns? When? She gazed at Lippy's unconscious form. The words spoken during that childhood game so long ago came back to her:

*Hey, that isn't fair.*

*You're right, Lippy. It was a dirty trick. But you should always be on guard.*

*Even against your friends?*

*Especially against your friends, Lippy. It's easy to be on guard against your enemies.*

"You're a fraud, David," murmured Myrna gently. "You were never on guard against your friends."

She left the room quickly.

Lipman regained consciousnes, and with his remaining strength crawled to the phone. He called Security.

"Myrna Lu . . . just left the penthouse. . . . Find her . . . put as many men as you can on it. . . . She has a cassette that can break the conspiracy wide open. . . . Get it. . . . Kill her."

He collapsed just as the stretcher-bearers arrived.

# 28

*Contact someone in government you can trust to get you to Damascus.*

Hafez' words.

Myrna hurried along the Avenue of the Americas in search of a recording shop for a reel of tape. She'd make the copy in her apartment.

*Who in government still untouched? With enough power to get her to Damascus?*

There were a few senators, incorruptible. But none powerful enough to get her through.

*Who, then?*

Her eyes glittered. There *was* someone. How could he refuse?

*Who but the president of the United States.*

She laughed sardonically at the irony of it.

The cab dropped her in front of her apartment building at the corner of Sixty-sixth Street and Third Avenue. She'd bought two cassettes to be on the safe side. Two copies. Each to be concealed in a different place. She'd take the original with her. In case the experts might question the validity of the copy.

She greeted the doorman. It occurred to her that he seemed nervous; ill at ease. He was always so friendly—deferential.

She shrugged away her nervousness.

The self-service elevator let her out on the fifteenth floor. She walked silently along the carpeted corridor to apartment 1504. Hers.

She paused to feel at the lock across which she'd stretched an invisible hair. A usual precaution.

It was not there.

Whoever was inside must have heard the elevator door open. He—they—whoever—would be waiting for her *now*. If she did not enter, he—they—would investigate.

She heard the voices: whispers, indistinguishable.

More than one.

She ran silently along the carpeted floor and hid herself in an alcove just as her door opened.

Silence. Then: "Must have been a tenant." Pause. The door closed.

She moved out of the niche and was startled to find a man standing outside her door.

The man was just as surprised to see her. He reached into his coat pocket. Myrna knew what he was reaching for.

She spun around and raced down the corridor toward the staircase. She didn't look back; she didn't think he would risk a shot. Her only concern was to get through the stairway door before he reached her.

The man was slow; a lumbering giant. Myrna

whipped around the corner to the staircase with seconds to spare.

She waited for him behind the door.

He came charging through the door, but stopped to peer down the stairwell. Myrna leaped. Her feet caught him in the back of the neck, catapulting him over the rail onto the cement landing below. He lay still, his skull crushed.

Myrna returned to the corridor and paused at her door; she'd take the other one by surprise.

The man inside heard the knock. Expecting his partner, he opened the door. His eyes widened in shock at the sight of her.

Myrna split the man's face open. He bellowed like a wounded animal and groped for her blindly.

From behind, with the side of her hand, Myrna severed his jugular. He tumbled to the rug, bleeding to death.

The room was a shambles. Everything was ripped apart, her recording device smashed.

She realized Lippy had somehow sounded the alarm. She'd never be able to return to her apartment. But there was one thing she had to do.

She locked the door and made her way along the corridor to the elevator.

The doorman was in the vestibule when Myrna reached him. The surprised look on his face changed to one of dismay when Myrna asked: "Why did you let those two men in my apartment?"

"What . . . what two men?" he stammered.

"One with a crushed skull and the other with a broken neck. Those two men. They were whole when you let them in."

He stared at this tiny woman in disbelief. How could she . . . ?

He discovered that she could, when her knee ripped

into his crotch, his testes never again to perform their function.

She left him groveling.

No time to make copies of the tape.

Later.

Myrna caught a plane to Washington after inquiring about Lipman's condition.

Not good. If he lived through the night, maybe . . .

Speed was everything now. Yet in the swiftness of the planning, precautions could not be overlooked. Copies of the tape—that was mandatory. Her plan to meet with the president was only the first step, the prelude, but it had to be handled delicately, craftily. He had to be made to understand that when the conspiracy was revealed, the label of traitor could not be traced to him but to the fanatacism of the others.

His insurance policy.

Self-protection.

Had the conspirators not brought him to the brink of disaster?

And wasn't his name left out of the tape?

She would make him a hero. He would grasp her logic.

The son of a bitch!

## Washington, D.C.

It was past midnight when Myrna checked into the Mayflower.

A hundred-dollar tip to the bellman brought her the necessary recording equipment.

She made two copies; one was placed in the hotel vault, the other in a box at the bus station.

Now to wake up the president.

# 29

## Damascus, Syria

Klaus Wagner and company, bound and strung together by wire, their mouths sealed with adhesive, sat motionless. At the slightest movement the wire cut into their flesh; the gags muffling their cries of pain. Blood draining from the engraved swastikas on their foreheads dripped into their eyes and coursed down their cheeks until crusted.

They were not a pretty sight.

They sat through the night. Sleepless. Numb. Lacerated from involuntary movements.

Chain reaction pain.

General Marley was unable to control his sphincter. The neighbor on each side of him was unable to avoid being dampened.

Klaus Wagner defecated with a frightening roar.

They stank. They ached. They hated.

In the morning, they heard the porter running his vacuum in the corridor; the chambermaids gossiping.

*Why didn't they come in?*

The prisoners couldn't call out; they couldn't move. They didn't know they were not to be disturbed.

The switchboard operator was puzzled. There were several calls for General Marley and she could not seem to get a ring. She notified the manager who, together with his assistant, went to investigate.

The sign on the door told them that the general was not to be disturbed. The manager checked his watch. It was close to noon. He looked for help from his assistant.

The assistant shrugged. "It says do not disturb."

"But something is wrong with the telephone," said the manager. "The calls may be important."

"It is also important that he not be disturbed."

"That is very true."

They stood for a moment contemplating a course of action. Then the manager said, "If we entered quietly it could not possibly be disturbing."

"I agree with that."

"Then let us enter quietly. Your key, please."

"I do not have a key, sir."

"You should have brought a key."

"I am sorry."

The manager snapped his finger at a chambermaid. "Open this door, please."

She came over. "It says do not disturb."

"I know. Open the door, please."

"But . . ."

"Open the door please . . . quietly."

She opened the door; they stepped into the foyer silently.

They were greeted by muffled moans from the sitting room and an overpowering stench.

The manager and his assistant retched.

The police investigation revealed that David Ring had never left the prison. Therefore General Marley and the others were mistaken.

General Marley was in the throes of hysteria as he and the other conspirators argued with the police officials in their hospital rooms. They were not mistaken. *It was David Ring who inflicted their punishment.*

*But how could that be? David Ring had never left the prison,* the officials argued.

*Yet he did! He did!* The conspirators argued back.

*If he left the prison why did he return? Why did he not flee?*

The victims swore it was David Ring. They raved, ranted in pain and humiliation.

The prefect shrugged. Must have been a Jewish gang, he deduced. One Jew could not inflict so much mayhem on so many.

*Besides, David Ring never left the prison.*

*But it was David Ring!*

The prefect left the hospital in disgust while the doctors continued to treat the wounds of the conspirators. The doctor told them there would be scars.

Only death would heal their humiliation.

# 30

## Washington, D.C.

The president of the United States was awakened at
1:30 A.M. by the magic word: *Lipman.* Transmitted
by telephone from Myrna to layers of lower echelon
to William Stoll, the president's chief of staff.

"Where are you?" asked Stoll.

Myrna told him.

"Stay on the line."

Two minutes. Then: "Yes?" Sleepily.

"Mr. President?"

"Yes?"

"My name is Myrna Lu, assistant to David Ring.
Less than three hours ago I shot the traitor, Julius
Lipman."

Gasp. Long pause. Stoll listened on the extension.

"Are you still with me?" she asked.

Weakly: "Yes . . ."

Myrna went on. "I have in my possession a tape of a certain meeting held at Lake George. It speaks for itself. I'll play it for you."

The president listened, stricken. The chief of staff, grim. He'd been alerted by the organization to the tape's existence. It had to be destroyed. Lipman's last directive.

"I have two copies concealed for my protection," Myrna continued. "If you want to save your neck, Mr. President, make the necessary arrangements for *Air Force One* to fly us to Damascus. Now! I'll see that you get full credit for discovering the tape. In the eyes of the world you'll be a hero. Otherwise, a traitor. No double-cross, Mr. President. Our conversation is being taped."

The president cast a look of pain at Stoll, searching for a decision. He got a nod from the chief.

"Very . . . well." His voice cracked. "I'll notify Andrews Air Force Base."

"No. I want the plane flown to Dulles. We'll leave from there. Bigger crowds. No military. Meet you in an hour."

She hung up and murmured, "It'll soon be over, David."

The president of the United States looked as if he might collapse. "What do we do?" he sobbed.

William Stoll was already doing it. First he placed a call to check on Lipman.

Dead.

Next, he called Damascus and was put through to General Marley.

The president got on the phone, blubbering wildly until Stoll took the phone from his trembling hand and told Marley what had happened.

*Hold.* A conference of the conspirators.

Then the decision: *Play for time.*

*Myrna Lu must not leave the country.*

Myrna needed help; someone to share her secret; someone who would deliver the tape in the event they disposed of her. Her Washington contacts were no longer operative.

Who?

*Martin Simon—ex-attorney general.*

She'd heard about his resignation; knew that his character was above reproach.

Within fifteen minutes the hotel bellman supplied her with Simon's unlisted phone number.

It was 2:00 A.M. when Myrna woke Martin Simon. She played the tape for him over the phone; told him where the other copies and the taped phone conversation were hidden should anything go wrong.

Simon listened, stunned.

*The director of the FBI listened on an interconnect.*

Myrna addressed an envelope to Martin Simon and in it she placed two keys. One for the box in the hotel vault; the other for the locker in the bus station.

She took the elevator down to the lobby, purchased a stamp at the desk and dropped the envelope in the mailbox. A deep breath. David would be safe.

The cab headed for Dulles, and Myrna leaned back, exhausted, utterly spent. She closed her eyes, and for the first time in days she allowed herself to drift. Suddenly, she sat up. She experienced a strangely persistent disquiet. *Something was wrong!* But what? Had she made an error? She probed. Something *done* or something *not* done? What? She sat forward, her mind working feverishly. What mistake? Where? When?

The taxi began to approach the airport. She could

see the outline of the president's plane in the far corner of the field. Huge and fully lighted.

The cab was waved on by Security according to directives.

Myrna trembled; her mind probing relentlessly. Something. Something . . .

*The bellman!*

*How was he able to get Martin's unlisted number?*

*He had to have had help!*

*Help in government!*

She issued a command to the taxi driver and the cab's tires screamed as it made a speeding U-turn.

Myrna berated herself ruthlessly for her carelessness.

The bellman looked at her in surprise.

"Come with me," Myrna said. "I'd like you to bring my bags down."

What bags? he said to himself. She only had a small overnight case. What was she up to?

He didn't have long to wait for an answer.

Myrna closed the door behind her and silently twisted the night latch. The bag was there, on the bed. It hadn't been on the bed when she left the room a short time ago. She remembered. She'd left it in the wardrobe.

"Is that it?" said the bellman with a crooked grin.

"You ought to know," said Myrna softly. "You left it there. When you searched it."

The grin was gone. "Why do you say that?"

"Isn't it true?"

"I don't know what you're talking about." He took the bag and started for the door.

"How did you get Martin Simon's phone number?"

The bellman paused, then looked over his shoulder. There was that grin again. "Tricks of the trade." He swivelled his head back to the door and reached for the doorknob.

Myrna took a measured step, then feet together, vaulted. Her spike heels rammed the bellman in the small of the back, hammering him against the door.

He crumpled to the floor like a broken doll. He moaned in anguish. Limp but conscious.

Myrna clamped his throat with her powerful hands. "Now you tell me who gave you Martin Simon's phone number."

He had breath enough to tell her it was the FBI. Also that they were waiting for her at Dulles. Also that Simon's apartment was under surveillance. *Also that the envelope containing the keys had been removed from the mailbox.* "You're a dead Chink," he gasped. Then he fainted.

Myrna ripped off the bellman's jacket and saw that his lung was probably punctured. He'd live. Maybe. She called for an ambulance.

3:00 A.M. *The president slept soundly. Secure. Good dreams. Had not the FBI agents destroyed the tapes? And would not the girl be intercepted at Dulles? And the original tape confiscated?*

His rosy dream was shattered by the jangling of the telephone.

"Mr. President," said the chief of staff. "Miss Lu has evaded the net. I have called a special meeting of the Security Council at which time we will chart a course of action. Don't worry, Mr. President. She won't live to use that tape. See you in a half hour. At the meeting."

The president removed his immense bulk from the bed. He tried to remain calm. His desperate thoughts turned to self-preservation. Survival. Didn't the girl say, "If you want to save your neck. . . . ?" Which meant there was a way out for him. There was nothing in the tape to connect him with the conspiracy. An innocent bystander. A victim. An unwitting tool. All he had to do was go along with the girl and he could be a hero. The savior of the country. Instead of just a lackey for Wagner and company.

He dressed hurriedly, his heart thumping at the prospect of the change of events; his mind searching for a plan of action.

*The girl. He must find her before they did.*

He called down to the Secret Service. "Pick up my car and park it two blocks south. I'll be waiting for you in the Rose Garden."

He was intercepted by Stoll, his chief of staff. "Too late for you to be out joyriding, Mr. President," said his chief. There was an edge to his voice.

Together they went to the council meeting.

The president sat at the head of the table.

Alone.

Myrna placed a call to Martin Simon from a street pay phone. "I have the tape," she told him. "I'm on my way to your place. Don't leave the building. You're under surveillance. I'll try to get a cab."

*The car swung from around the corner and mounted the curb stopping flush against the framed glass door of the phone booth.*

*Caged.*

Blinded by the glare of the headlights Myrna did not see the two men get out, but she knew they were there. With their guns drawn.

There was nothing she could do but wait to be taken.

Stoll was informed of the prize.

Rendezvous: A motel in Arlington on the other side of the river.

William Stoll shared two traits common to his fore-bears in the Hitler regime. He was a good questioner and an exotic torturer. Qualities developed over the years as a CIA cover. He was proud of his accomplishments in the field.

He arrived at the motel by car and hurried to room 112. The shades were drawn but there was a light inside. The door opened at his knock.

She was there, a bruise on the cheekbone; bound hand and foot to the bed. Her captors stood by, their jackets off. They wore pistols in shoulder holsters.

Stoll spotted Myrna's handbag on a chair. He dumped the contents out on the floor and felt around inside.

No cassette.

He swung his look at the two agents.

"Our orders were not to open it," said one. "We didn't search her person either."

Stoll nodded. "Wait outside."

The chief straddled a chair. He stroked his small mustache, then lit a cigarette. "Where is it?" he asked.

"Where is what?" answered Myrna.

"The cassette."

"What cassette?"

He sucked hard on the cigarette and drew the smoke deep into his lungs. When he let it out it swirled about his face as he spoke.

"You might as well tell me where you've hidden it," he said. "It will never reach Damascus in time anyway."

"Then why do you want it?"

"It's not a nice thing to have around."

"You're sensitive."

"No. Just careful."

"It is a nasty little item, isn't it?"

No reply.

Myrna continued. "Can you imagine what would happen if the world listened to it? Even after the takeover. You fellows would be in quite a mess."

"That's why I want it."

"I can understand that."

William Stoll got up from the chair and snuffed his cigarette by letting it drop on the carpet and grinding it with the toe of his shoe. He then went to the bed and stripped Myrna naked, examining each item she wore. Shoes, pantyhose, seams in the clothing . . .

When he leaned over to examine her hair she spat in his face.

He said nothing. Simply used his handkerchief and grinned.

Myrna new what was coming. *The lit cigarette pressed to the nipples. If that didn't work then the wire coat hanger inserted into the vagina as far as it could go with resistance. After that the upward pressure.*

Stoll continued to grin as he lighted another cigarette. Same expression when he waved out the match and dropped it to the floor. Now the grin widened so that his teeth showed. He stood alongside her; took a deep pull at the cigarette to get a bright, glowing head. He examined it for a brief moment, blew off the ash from the tip, and, holding the end between thumb and forefinger of one hand, leaned over and cupped her small breast with the other.

Standard procedure.

He brought the glowing tip down slowly so that she could feel the heat as a prelude. It worked.

"You win," said Myrna.

He nodded. "I knew I would."

"It's in one of the pillows on the bed in my room at the Mayflower."

Pause. "You hadn't checked out?"

"No."

He gave her a hard look.

"It's there," she said.

He went to the door and beckoned to his agents. "One of you come with me." To the other he said, "Stay with her and wait for my call."

After they left, the remaining agent locked the door from the inside.

He was a big man. About six-four, two hundred and sixty pounds of flesh, bone and muscle. He sweated a lot.

He sweated more when he gazed at Myrna's naked loveliness. He looked at his watch. There was time.

Myrna recognized the symptoms. She began to undulate ever so subtly. She heard his breath quicken.

He undressed quickly; sweat pouring. His hands shook as he untied her feet. Clumsily, he tried to mount her.

"I can help," she said. Her voice low and throaty. "If you untie my hands."

He was on top of her, slobbering.

"We don't have much time," she said.

"Yeah," he grunted.

"You'll never make it. Let me help."

In a frenzy he released her hands.

She raised her legs. He thought it was an invitation. He was so wrong. Her powerful legs lashed around his throat fracturing his Adam's apple. At the same time, she slammed the heel of her hand against his chin with such force that his neck snapped with an audible crack.

He rolled off the bed; blood oozing out of his mouth. He was dead.

Myrna got dressed, removed the dead agent's gun from its holster and the car keys from his trousers pocket. She lifted the phone receiver and dialed for the correct time.

She let the receiver hang. The recorded voice of the operator would make her announcement every fifteen seconds. Anyone calling in would get a busy signal. *That was the time Myrna needed. When Stoll called in.*

Precious time.

Myrna drove the agent's car to the phone booth where she'd been picked up.

The cassette was there.

Under the phone box where she had left it.

# *31*

If Myrna failed to deliver the tape in Damascus, Martin Simon knew his days were numbered. There wasn't anybody in the United States with enough clout to challenge the conspirators. The takeover was too far advanced.

He stared out the window at the darkness that now enfolded Washington. His apartment was on the fourteenth floor, affording a good view of the capital's skyline, especially with the lights out in his living room. He stood there in the dark, dressed in a bathrobe, no slippers on his feet, watching as a grayish purple began to impose itself on the black sky. Vague outlines of cloud wisps could be discerned.

He had been looking at Washington's skyline most of this night. As he'd been doing the many nights since his horrifying meeting with the president and the secretary of state. What sleep he managed was fitful, subject to sudden torments and awakenings. His pillow was always damp from his nervous perspiration.

*Oh, God! It was beyond belief!*

Insanity beyond comprehension.

The ex-attorney general turned his gaze to the stakeout below. A single man in a dark sedan. The man smoking. Waiting. Constant surveillance, Myrna had said.

As he looked, there appeared the shadow of a woman, moving stealthily toward the sedan.

Myrna?

She crouched at the rear of the car on the curbside. From his vantage point it seemed she was letting the air out of a tire.

The stakeout heard the sound and got out to investigate. A cigarette dangled from his lips.

He didn't have a chance. From where Simon watched, Myrna's motions were a blur of destructive speed. The man fell like a rock.

Myrna dragged him to the front seat and set him behind the wheel. His head lolled as if he were dozing. No longer smoking. She removed his weapon and crossed swiftly to the entrance of the apartment building.

Martin Simon let her in. They had never met before. He greeted her with: "You're pretty good."

"You saw it?"

He nodded. "All I've been doing the past few nights is staring out the window. Searching for a hope, I guess. Then you came along."

He crossed to the bar. "I don't know about you, Miss Lu, but I need a drink."

"We don't have much time, Mr. Simon. You'd

better get dressed and think of a way to get us out of here."

"I'm not very good at thinking these days." He tossed off a shot of whiskey and followed it with another. "I'll do the best I can." He started for the bedroom, his thin, wiry body beginning to overcome its lassitude. "Be ready in a jiffy."

She called out to him. "How about the Dutch ambassador? Is there anything he can do to help?"

"No way," said Simon from inside the bedroom. "Pouches are no longer sacrosanct. Nobody leaves without a thorough search; they'll break into embassies if they have to. Ambassadors can't even place a call to their capitals without being monitored. We're in a police state, Miss Lu."

Silence.

"Miss Lu?"

"Yes?"

"Any other ideas?"

Long silence.

Simon came out of the bedroom and found her weeping. He crossed to her; held her in his arms, cradling her as one would a child. Could this be the same woman who had put away the agent? All the pent-up fury and tension gave way to tears and sobs. "Oh, David . . . David . . ." she moaned.

He let her cry out her anguish. And when she was through, he brushed the tears that remained on her cheek.

"Myrna," he said softly. "There is still a hope."

Her dark eyes brightened.

"Could be," he said as he crossed to the phone. "It just could be."

He started to dial.

The phone rang in the dark bedroom of the commander of Andrews Air Force Base. General Turley woke slowly, still drugged by the alcohol he used to forget his travail. A blessed panacea he'd discovered since the Great Upheaval. It eased the shame. The shame of being part of it.

The telephone rang again. Stridently. He turned on his reading lamp and stared myopically at the bedside clock. It told him it was 4:00 A.M.

*Who the hell . . .*

He fumbled for the phone. "Yes?" he said in a hoarse voice.

"Who?" He rose on one elbow, blinking at the light, licking his drug-dry lips.

Martin Simon's story finally penetrated.

*My God! A way out!*

Slowly, General Turley replaced the receiver and with a trembling hand poured himself a glass of water. He got it to his lips by using both hands and gulped it down. It had the sobering effect of black coffee and his mind began to clear.

He dialed a number. It seemed to ring forever. The general cursed. If he wasn't there . . .

Click. Pause. A cracked voice: "Hello . . ."

"Get your ass over here on the double!" said Turley.

He cradled the phone, moved quickly to the bathroom and emptied his bladder.

He stared at his bloated, red-eyed image in the mirror as he'd so often done. The reflection never changed. But now . . .

He stepped under a hot, steaming shower. The soap washed away his stench. Then he turned on the cold water. The icy spray tingled his blood; his heart raced.

*Hope!*

By the time he finished dressing, Colonel Harkavy had arrived. Unshaven; eyes still filled with sleep.

He was a small, wiry man of forty with a brush hair-cut.

"I want you to round up a crew to fly us to Damascus," said Turley.

"What?"

"In a B-52."

"You gotta be kiddin', Mort."

"Now!"

"Damascus?"

"Damnit, you want out, don't you?"

"Yes, but . . ."

"So do I! I just heard the goddamndest story—it'll set the world on its ear. We don't have too much time, Harky. You gotta round up men we can trust." Then he added, bitterly. "There aren't many around these days."

"Jesus, Mort . . ."

"Get crackin'!"

The colonel grinned. "Like old times, Mort."

The colonel dashed out the door and the general picked up the phone and dialed. Then: "General Turley, here. Put me through to Bill Stoll." Pause. "I don't give a shit if the Security Council is in session. Put me through or I'll have your neck!"

Stoll lifted the phone in the cabinet room. Liaison gave him the message.

He scowled. What the hell could he want?

"What's up, Turley?" he said. "We're in the middle of a meeting."

"Remember when you had me send *Air Force One* across to Dulles?"

"So?"

"Something about picking up a girl? You seemed to want her real bad. Right?"

Stoll held his breath.

"Still with me, Bill?"

"Keep talking."

Pause. "The Dutch ambassador picked her up with Martin Simon. They're on their way to Dulles. A KLM 747 is warming up."

General Turley, happy with his lie, hung up and hurried out to his car.

# 32

The chief of staff went into action.
*Roadblock.*
*Helicopter search.*
*Dulles surveillance.*
He'd have them *trapped!* . . . he thought.

It was Lipman who had appointed William Stoll chief of staff. He had done well.
In the New Order Stoll's future was assured.
*Provided he could prevent the tape and the girl from reaching Damascus. She had already outwitted him once.*
A shudder ran through his frame as he sat waiting in his office. What if a radio station ran the tape?
Who would dare!
Some clandestine station?

No. They'd find it before the damage could be done. And yet . . .

He dismissed the thought. The organization was strong. The roadblock, helicopter surveillance—both working in unison under his direction with perfect efficiency.

But he could not just sit and wait. He had to be there. To take charge. To search. . . . A clawing fear gripped him.

He didn't wait for his car to be brought around. Instead he raced out to the parking lot. He did not feel the harsh, diagonal sheets of rain that pounded from the dark sky; he did not notice that his raincoat —unbuttoned—had fallen away, the storm drenching him to the skin. His fear swept everything aside but the immediate crisis.

The car sped through the rain, the wipers lashing the water from the windshield.

We are irresistible, his mind was telling him. Invincible. Already the world was being apportioned.

Swish . . . swish . . . went the wipers.

Governments falling into line. A question of time. Less than forty-eight hours.

Swish . . . swish . . .

The trial . . . the tape . . .

Everything reduced to the tape!

The roadblock loomed ahead.

A captain approached the car and the chief rolled down his window. A questioning look.

No, the block had not been penetrated.

Good.

The helicopter was contacted. "No, sir. No sign of the ambassador's vehicle. Poor visibility."

The rain continued without letup. The chief sat in his car and shivered. . . . They had to come this way. . . . If they escaped the roadblock, they'd have been intercepted at Dulles. . . . If only the goddamn rain would stop.

Traffic was intermittent. Halted and examined. 4:30 A.M.

The chief's mind continued to ramble. What if she got out? What were the alternatives?

No alternatives.

Sit tight.

She had no way out.

5:00 A.M. First light.

General Turley pulled up in front of Martin Simon's apartment building and raced into the lobby.

On the opposite side, the body of the stakeout agent sat behind the wheel in the sedan, its head still fixed at a strange angle.

The dead man's relief pulled up behind the other car, got out and walked to the driver's side.

One look was enough.

He raced back to his car and hit the radio just as General Turley, Martin Simon and Myrna emerged from the lobby.

The agent spotted them. He recognized the general. What was he doing with the woman? And Martin Simon? The two of them apprehended? Could be. But why wasn't Security in on it? Why the commander of Andrews? Hell, the way they were doing things these days.

He tried to raise the chief of Security.

*"Hold on. Trying to locate."*

*Should he follow the general's car?*

The agent shivered. They'd have his head.

*"Hold, please."*

William Stoll took heart, for the rain stopped and

221

the mist cleared. His shortwave crackled with a report from the helicopter.

No sign of the ambassador's car.

He raised Dulles. All KLM planes temporarily restrained.

He called Andrews.

"General Turley left the base, sir. Twenty minutes ago."

"Have him call me."

SECURITY LIAISON: "Hold please. Still trying to raise the chief."

AGENT: "Where the hell is he?"

SECURITY LIAISON: "Hold please."

AGENT: "Shit!"

General Turley's car sped through the front gate of the base past the two guards. Past Administration, Recreation, hangars, without slowing down.

The buildings were still dark.

At a far runway the imposing silhouette of a B-52 sat waiting, its engines warming.

The general's car came to a screeching halt at the edge of the runway just as a jeep raced up with the message for the general to call the chief of staff.

Turley nodded.

The messenger watched the group climb into the plane and wondered what it was all about. He got back into his jeep and reported to the guard at the gate.

The guard lifted the phone and placed a call to William Stoll.

SECURITY LIAISON: "Still trying to ring the chief."

AGENT: "The hell with it. Get me William Stoll."

SECURITY LIAISON: "I can't connect you from this end. He's in transit. Have your operator do it."

AGENT: "Thanks for nothing."

The agent placed his call. He glanced at his watch. *Shit. Twenty-seven minutes.*

William Stoll sat huddled in his car, his brain striving for answers that weren't there. He had to move. Where the hell was Turley? Damnit, why didn't he call?

He lifted the phone to call the base.

How often does it happen opposite calls are made at the same moment resulting in busy signals?

Not often. Yet, mathematically possible.

The guard at Andrews and Stoll got busy signals at the same moment.

An instant later when Stoll hung up, the agent got through to him. He told him about the dead agent. Then ended with: "Another thing, sir. I wanted to tell chief of Security about it. We should have been informed about General Turley."

Stoll's eyes rolled. "What about General Turley?"

"He picked up Martin Simon and the girl."

*A bolt of lightning!*

*Blood pounded in his ears!*

He hung up on the agent, spun his car around and headed for Andrews. *Turley. The son of a bitch! Fuckin' traitor!*

He drove like a wild man, as he put in a call to the base.

"I've been trying to reach you," the guard at the gate told the frantic Stoll. "General Turley took off in a B-52. He had two people with him. A man and a girl."

So, they'd gone. He was too late.

*Strange reaction.*

*He grinned.*

*Then broke into a fit of hysterical laughter.*

# 33

They sat in silence, the three of them. Their individual thoughts on different wavelengths.

Myrna yearned to see David whole again.

Simon saw the world reconstructed. Affirmation of the human spirit.

Turley felt his soul redeemed.

And the giant plane pounded on toward Damascus, its huge engines leaving vapor trails, as if spelling out the word *hope*.

Myrna, pragmatic Myrna, broke the silence. "General," she said. "I think the radio operator should try to raise President Dasat in Damascus."

Simon nodded his agreement.

Turley waited for her reasons.

"I think you should talk to him; to tell him we're on our way with earth-shaking news."

225

"Makes sense," said Turley. "We might even play part of the tape for him."

He signaled the operator.

*After a few minutes, the radio operator announced that he had President Dasat on the phone. Then the first shot from the Phantom jet's cannon ripped into the tail of the B-52.*

*The second shot exploded the cockpit.*

*The fuselage tumbled end over end like the giant vane of an ancient windmill.*

*Down.*

*Down.*

*Down.*

*And Myrna cried: "Oh, David!"*

The pilot of the Phantom watched the tumbling plane until it plunged into the sea. Then he made radio contact with William Stoll and announced: "Mission accomplished."

He headed back to Andrews Air Force Base.

# PART THREE

# *34*

A small Israeli missile launch carrying a dozen hard-faced men left the Port of Haifa and headed out to sea showing no lights.

Four hours later it hove to, opposite a Mediterranean shoreline barely visible in the distance. On the bridge, the captain signaled with a wink from his torch.

A light from the shore blinked its reply twice.

A rubber raft was put over the side and twelve armed men got aboard. Swiftly but silently they stroked for shore.

One of them, staring intently towards the approaching beach, was Major Benn Yussid, broad-shouldered strike leader of the Mossad Aliyah Bet, the Israeli Secret Service.

Three jeeps were parked in a row on the beach.

Each contained four Syrian military uniforms. Also an assortment of weapons.

Major Benn Yussid looked at his watch: 2:45. On schedule as planned.

But would it work?

## Damascus, Syria

The crowd in the square in front of the Supreme Court Building stood tense and silent as the testimony spilled out of the loudspeakers.

Soldiers with automatic weapons stood guard at the entrances.

Inside, cordoned off from the spectators, sat the Nazi conspirators. With patches on their foreheads to conceal the engraved swastikas.

Fredericks, the thin, tense FBI director, stood in the witness dock as the prosecutor weaved the noose that he hoped to place around David Ring's neck.

The incriminating letter bearing David's fingerprints, typed on David's machine. So attested to by the experts. The damaging copy outlining the details of the destruction at the U.N. The original purportedly mailed to the Israeli Secret Service.

The noose: drawn tighter . . . tighter . . .

David sat at the defense table marveling at the neatness of the frame. *What else did they have?*

*If Myrna didn't come, then what?*

*Then it was up to Hafez.*

"How did you get this copy?" the attorney general asked the witness.

"My agent photographed it from the original," answered Fredericks.

The attorney general faced the court. "Honorable sirs, I offer the letter in evidence."

Hafez rose. "Objection, honorable sirs. The witness' agent has not testified to the accuracy of the witness' statements. The so-called 'facts' can only be classified as hearsay."

The chief justice gazed down at the witness. "Is your agent present to verify your statements?"

"No, honorable sir. She was killed shortly before the destruction of the United Nations Building. We found the letter in her effects."

The justice turned to Hafez. "Mr. Ameer, since the agent is unable to appear, and since the experts have testified that the letter is a photographic copy typed on the defendant's machine and from an original bearing the defendant's fingerprints, I must accept it for what it is worth. I therefore overrule your objection and permit the copy into evidence." He turned to the attorney general. "Continue."

"No further questions."

"You may cross-examine," said the justice to Hafez.

Hafez began. "Mr. Fredericks, your agent's name—was it Anna Thornton?"

"Yes, sir."

"She was on the payroll of the FBI?"

"Yes, sir."

"Was she also on the payroll of the president of the United States?"

"I wouldn't know."

"You say that you discovered the letter among Anna Thornton's effects."

"Yes, sir."

"With the defendant's fingerprints on it?"

"That is correct."

"Is it possible to transfer a fingerprint from one object to another?"

"Yes. It's possible."

"Would the FBI laboratories be familiar with that process?"

"Yes."

"Has the FBI ever performed that operation?"

"Yes. Experimentally."

"For what purpose?"

"To see if it could be done."

"Did the FBI transfer David Ring's fingerprints on the photographic copy of the letter—experimentally?"

"No. We did not."

"Do you know that of your own knowledge?"

"I don't know what you mean."

"I mean could the transfer have been made without your knowledge?"

Pause. "I imagine it could. If you're inferring that Anna Thornton delivered the letter to the lab together with a copy of the defendant's fingerprints, that's nonsense. She wouldn't have had time."

Softly. "I wasn't inferring anything, Mr. Fredericks. . . . What makes you certain that it was Anna Thornton who photographed the letter?"

"That was her assignment."

"*Then you knew the original existed before it was mailed!*"

"Of course not. Her assignment was to gather any evidence that might reveal David Ring's activities."

"You were suspicious of David Ring's activities?"

"Yes, sir."

"Activities such as building children's hospitals, churches, children's summer camps? Activities endeavoring to inhibit terrorism around the world? His charitable activities—these aroused the FBI's suspicions?"

"No, sir."

"Then tell the honorable court which of David Ring's activities *was* suspicious in your mind's eye."

"His close ties with Israel."

"Ah, that made the FBI suspicious?"

"Yes, sir."

"Tell me, sir. Did you assign agents to gather material against Senators Morgan, Hartley, Grunland, Barritz, Langer; Congressmen Forsythe, Harris, Kelly, Lindstrom, former Attorney General Martin Simon?"

"Of course not."

"But they had very close ties with Israel. That is a known fact, is it not?"

No answer.

"Isn't it a fact, sir, that you, in the company of others, conspired to *get* David Ring? Even to go so far as to falsify evidence?"

ATTORNEY GENERAL: "I object! The question implies that the witness is guilty of a crime."

CHIEF JUSTICE: "Would it not be to your interest to have the witness dissipate the implication?"

ATTORNEY GENERAL: (a grin) "I withdraw my objection."

CHIEF JUSTICE: "The witness will answer the question."

HAFEZ: "With the honorable court's permission I would like to repeat the question. . . . Isn't it a fact, Mr. Fredericks, that you, in the company of others, conspired to *get* David Ring? Even to go so far as to falsify evidence?"

"No, sir."

"A week before the disaster at the United Nations —on a Friday—did you not attend a meeting in the home of Anna Thornton in Lake George, New York, with Klaus Wagner . . ." He turned to face the conspirators. ". . . Senator Franklyn, Reverend Carson, Secretary Brandon and General Marley?"

Pause. Then: "No, sir."

"Your answer then is that you attended no such meeting. Is that correct?"

"That is correct."

Hafez crossed to the defense table and from a box, removed a cassette. He then returned to the dock. "If I told you that here in my hand is a cassette containing a tape of that meeting secretly made by Anna Thornton, outlining a conspiracy against David Ring and the world, would your answer still be the same?"

The conspirators sat forward in their chairs, their faces taut with fear.

Fredericks' quick mind considered the possibility that the tape was genuine—and rejected it.

*Impossible.*

*He would have known.*

*A trick. An old one.*

But doubts intruded against his better judgment.

What if—somehow—the tape had been delivered . . .

"And was not Anna Thornton murdered by one of your men because you feared she might reveal the substance of that meeting?" Hafez went on.

Beads of perspiration began to sprout on the FBI director's forehead. The figure of Hafez seemed to dance in front of him miasmically while the tape appeared to flow toward him, then ebb. He was surprised to hear how calmly he answered. "You have no such tape, Mr. Hafez."

Hafez grinned. "Not here in my hand, Mr. Fredericks. But I expect it momentarily. For one of Mr. Ring's associates found it where it was hidden—at Lake George." He tossed the cassette to David, then returned to Fredericks. "On what day was Miss Thornton assigned to David Ring?"

"It was a Sunday, I believe."

"And when was she killed?"

"The next day. Monday."

"Four days before the U.N. disaster?"

"That is correct."

"Then she must have photographed the letter at some time between the day of her assignment and the day she was murdered. Isn't that so?"

"Yes, sir."

"In order to photograph the letter it must have been on Mr. Ring's desk."

"I imagine so."

"When he wasn't present, naturally. When she saw the nature of the letter, she never called you about it?"

"No, sir."

"Don't you think that's strange?"

"Perhaps she didn't have time."

"She didn't have time to notify you that the U.N. Building was to be destroyed?"

No answer.

"Did you know Anna Thornton spent Sunday night with David Ring?"

"Not to my own knowledge."

"Did you know that Anna Thornton had lunch with David Ring on Monday, at a restaurant known as 21? We have witnesses to that effect."

"I wouldn't know."

"But you do know the time of day Anna Thornton was killed."

"Yes, sir."

"It was late Monday afternoon. Isn't that right?"

"Yes, sir."

"In the private elevator of the David Ring Building."

"I read the newspaper report of it."

"And during the night when she photographed the letter and all morning and most of that afternoon, Anna Thornton allegedly had in her possession the photographed letter and she never called you or spoke to you about it. You still think she didn't have, as you say, time to communicate with you? *To notify the FBI of an impending disaster?*"

"It's impossible—she didn't have the opportunity."

"Opportunity! Two hours at a luncheon and no oportunity to tell somebody—anybody—a policeman, the headwaiter, 'Here! take this letter to the FBI.' No opportunity?"

No answer.

"Isn't it a pity that Anna Thornton is not present to testify? So that she could tell this court why she never revealed the conspiracy to destroy the U.N. Building and its occupants?"

No answer.

"Sir—" Hafez' voice thundered. "—I submit that your agent, Anna Thornton, typed the letter on Mr. Ring's machine, on Mr. Ring's desk, while Mr. Ring slept. That she then photographed the letter and destroyed the original. That the next morning she handed you the film together with a set of Mr. Ring's fingerprints to be transferred to the paper. *And that afternoon you arranged to have her murdered.*"

The great hall boiled and the attorney general screamed his objections while the chief justice tried to make himself heard. Finally:

CHIEF JUSTICE: (sternly) "Mr. Ameer, do you intend to prove those accusations?"

HAFEZ: "With due respect, honorable sir, it is obvious that I cannot offer proof without Anna Thornton's presence. By the same token, the attorney general cannot offer proof of the legitimacy of the letter without Anna Thornton's presence. I therefore renew my objection to the letter in evidence, and move that the alleged evidence of conspiracy be stricken from the record and declared void."

The chief justice turned to his associates. Each

marked a slip of paper which the justice examined. He then pounded his gavel and announced: "Objection to the letter is sustained and further grant defendant's motion to strike, and I hereby declare the testimony of the witness, so far as it relates to the letter, be null and void."

David and Hafez exchanged warm smiles.

Now what? They knew the conspirators had more. *Direct examination of Carl Fredericks continued.*

ATTORNEY GENERAL: "I show you this reel of tape and ask you if contained therein is an accurate transcription of a conversation that took place between the Israeli ambassador and Major Benn Yussid, head of the Mossad, over the telephone in the ambassador's office, and between the ambassador and David Ring."

FREDERICKS: "That is correct."

ATTORNEY GENERAL: "Where did this taping take place?"

FREDERICKS: "A few doors from the embassy."

ATTORNEY GENERAL: "You were present at the time?"

FREDERICKS: "Yes, sir."

ATTORNEY GENERAL: (to the Court) "Honorable sirs, I request the clerk to mark this reel of tape for identification prior to its admission in evidence."

CHIEF JUSTICE: "So ordered."

CLERK: "State's Exhibit 'B.' So marked."

FREDERICKS: "Now, with the Court's permission, may I play the tape so that its content may assist you in your judgment?"

CHIEF JUSTICE: "So ordered."

There it was. The damning evidence. Spliced and falsified.

David listened. Despite his internal strength, it made him sick to his soul.

MAJOR YUSSID'S VOICE: "... *it calls for action, David. Klaus Wagner must be eliminated in order to insure the destruction of the U.N. ... Nothing must interfere. Please. I beg of you. See to it that Wagner is destroyed. Shalom.*"

AMBASSADOR'S VOICE: "*Well, David?*"

DAVID'S VOICE: "*Send a message to Major Benn Yussid. Tell him not to worry. The U.N. will be destroyed as planned. ... And as for Wagner, my agents will have him pinned down so that he will be unable to act. Tell him no one can stop us.*"

End of the tape.

ATTORNEY GENERAL: "I now offer this reel of tape in evidence."

HAFEZ: "Objection! No evidence has been adduced as to the tape's authenticity."

CHIEF JUSTICE: "Overruled. The witness has testified that the tape is an accurate transcription made in his presence. This is sufficient. The tape identified as State's Exhibit B is hereby admitted into evidence."

HAFEZ: "Then, honorable sir, I respectfully request an adjournment of this trial so that I may have time to secure an expert's opinion relevant to the authenticity of the tape."

CHIEF JUSTICE: "If I were to grant your request, and should your expert testify that the tape was a fraud, then the state—as a matter of right—should be given an opportunity to procure its own expert to counter your expert's opinion."

HAFEZ: "That is correct, honorable sir."

CHIEF JUSTICE: "It seems to me that this will only result in an abuse of time. I therefore take judicial notice of the fact that your expert will testify that the tape is a fraud and that it was tampered with. I will also take judicial notice that the state's expert will testify that the tape is authentic. As a result, we have gained nothing. Your request for adjournment is denied. You may cross-examine."

Hafez was stunned. It was an incredible ruling. David shook his head in disbelief. He turned to look at the media correspondents on their high perch. Their incredulity showed in their faces as they barked the news into their telephones.

Hafez stared long at Fredericks. How could he break him? Some trick or device, perhaps. But what?

HAFEZ: "Mr. Fredericks, you are presently the director of the FBI. Is that correct?"

FREDERICKS: "Yes, sir."

HAFEZ: "You testified that you were present at the taping. Was anyone else with you at the time?"

FREDERICKS: "Yes. A technician."

HAFEZ: "I assume he will corroborate your testimony?"

FREDERICKS: "He is not here, sir. He passed away."

HAFEZ: "Oh?"

FREDERICKS: "He suffered a heart attack shortly after the taping."

HAFEZ: "Most inconvenient, wouldn't you say?"

FREDERICKS: "Yes, sir. He would have confirmed the truth of my statements."

HAFEZ: "Or proven you a liar!"

ATTORNEY GENERAL: "Objection!"

HAFEZ: "Simply offering an alternative to the witness' contention of truth, honorable sir."

CHIEF JUSTICE: "Overruled."

HAFEZ: "You had a tap on the Israeli ambassador's telephone. And you had planted listening devices in his study. Why?"

FREDERICKS: "Standard procedure."

HAFEZ: "In all embassies?"

FREDERICKS: "Only those we don't trust."

HAFEZ: "Which ones are those?"

FREDERICKS: "That's highly classified information."

HAFEZ: "Yes. . . . How long before the destruction of the U.N. Building did Major Benn Yussid phone the Israeli ambassador?"

FREDERICKS: "About twelve hours."

HAFEZ: "In other words, the night before."

FREDERICKS: "Yes, sir."

HAFEZ: "That is when you taped the conversation?"

FREDERICKS: "Yes, sir."

HAFEZ: "Did you make an effort to immediately apprehend Mr. Ring?"

FREDERICKS: "Yes, sir. But by the time we got there he was gone."

HAFEZ: "When you learned of the plot why didn't you evacuate the U.N. and the surrounding area?"

FREDERICKS: (long pause) "I'll never forgive myself for not having done so. We weren't sure when the action was to take place. We thought the area was secure. We were mistaken. We underestimated Ring and the Israeli organization behind him."

HAFEZ: "Objection!"

CHIEF JUSTICE: "The scribe will strike the last sentence of the witness' testimony. . . . Proceed, Mr. Ameer."

HAFEZ: "Was there any other time that you taped a phone conversation between Major Benn Yussid and the ambassador?"

FREDERICKS: "No, sir. We have no record of any other phone conversation between the two."

HAFEZ: "But you are sure of the time of the taped phone call?"

FREDERICKS: "Yes, sir."

HAFEZ: "It was the night before the disaster?"

FREDERICKS: "Yes, sir."

HAFEZ: "And you just happened to be present at the taping at that time."

FREDERICKS: "Yes, sir."

HAFEZ: "The disaster took place on a Friday morning. You taped the phone conversation on Thursday night. What time was that?"

FREDERICKS: "About ten o'clock. Mr. Ring arrived about midnight."

Hafez went to the counsel table and removed a paper from his briefcase. He then returned with it to the dock to face Fredericks.

HAFEZ: (perusing the paper) "You are right, Mr. Fredericks. According to the overseas operator, Major Benn Yussid did call at about ten o'clock. (pause) *But it wasn't Thursday night. It was Monday night! Four days before the destruction of the U.N. Building!* (waving the paper) Do you wish to change your story, Mr. Fredericks?"

Fredericks' mouth fell open and his usually keen mind swirled in turmoil. Of course it was Monday night . . . but he could not admit that . . . they'd want to know why he had remained silent . . . and permitted the U.N.'s destruction. . . . *Brazen it out . . . his word against the word of a telephone operator . . . hint that she had been bribed. . . .*

HAFEZ: "Come, come, Mr. Fredericks. I ask you again. Do you wish to change your story? You may have forgotten what night it was, Mr. Fredericks. A human failing. It happened so long ago. It could have been Monday night, could it not? Think, Mr. Fredericks. We have much time. You had a great burden on your mind. Your agent, Anna Thornton, was murdered that Monday afternoon. It must have shocked you. And that very night the Israeli call came in and you lost track of time and you thought it was Thursday, a mere twelve hours before that horror at the U.N. Now think back a moment, and tell the honorable court what day the call was received."

*No answer.*

HAFEZ: "It was Monday, wasn't it Mr. Fredericks?"

*No answer.*

HAFEZ: "Of course it was Monday. And the call *was* taped as you have testified. But what was recorded was entirely different from what was admitted here in evidence. Actually, Mr. Fredericks, did not Major Benn Yussid warn David Ring that Klaus Wagner was plotting a dastardly deed in such a manner as to place the blame on Israel, timing it with Yassim Sivad's visit at the U.N.? That Major Benn Yussid pleaded in his message for David Ring to exert every effort to stop Sivad's appearance so that the plot—whatever it was—would be aborted? And, if necessary to prevent a terrible disaster, he suggested that David Ring destroy Klaus Wagner? Now, wasn't that the crux of the telephone call that you taped? And did you not have the tape doctored so that it would appear that David Ring was the conspirator?"

FREDERICKS: *"No!"*

HAFEZ: "But the call *was* received Monday night. Isn't that correct?"

*No answer. A gnawing fear.*

HAFEZ: *"Four days before the destruction of the U.N. And you did nothing to stop it?"*

FREDERICKS: (barely audible) "The call came in Thursday night."

HAFEZ: "Mr. Fredericks, you must be aware that all incoming calls to Washington from foreign lands are monitored and automatically recorded as to the exact time received and the parties involved. (waving the paper) Are you questioning the validity of the telephone company's recorder?"

ATTORNEY GENERAL: "Honorable sirs, I request the opportunity to examine the telephone company's certification."

HAFEZ: "I have not as yet offered it into evidence. The attorney general will have ample opportunity to examine the document at the proper time."

CHIEF JUSTICE: "Continue, Mr. Ameer."

HAFEZ: "I ask you again, Mr. Fredericks. Are you questioning the validity of the telephone company's recorder?"

FREDERICKS: "No."

HAFEZ: (waving the paper) "Then if the telephone company's recorder reveals that the call came in Monday night, and not Thursday, you will accept that as fact."

FREDERICKS: (long pause) "Yes. But I don't believe . . . that the recorder . . . will reveal that the call came in Monday night."

HAFEZ: "Will it reveal that the call came in Thursday night?"

FREDERICKS: "I don't know."

HAFEZ: "If it came in Thursday the recorder should reveal that fact, should it not?"

FREDERICKS: "Yes."

HAFEZ: "And you will accept that fact?"

FREDERICKS: "Yes."

HAFEZ: (waving the paper) "Will you now swear that according to the telephone company's records the call came in Thursday night?"

No answer. Hafez waited. Would this be the break? Finally.

CHIEF JUSTICE: "The witness will please answer the question."

FREDERICKS: "I . . . I would like . . . the question repeated."

HAFEZ: "Certainly. Will you swear that according to

243

the telephone company's records the call came in Thursday night?"

ATTORNEY GENERAL: "I now object to the question, honorable sirs. How can the witness swear to the records when he has not examined them?"

HAFEZ: "The witness has testified that he will accept the fact that if the call came in Thursday the recorder will reveal it. He has also testified that of his own knowledge the call came in Thursday. What better evidence is there than the automatic record of the call? Therefore why should the honorable attorney general object to the corroboration of the witness' statement? . . . Unless, honorable sirs, the witness is lying."

CHIEF JUSTICE: "Mr. Ameer, if you will offer the document in evidence I will take judicial notice of the accuracy of its contents."

HAFEZ: "Even should the document reveal that the call was made on Monday and not Thursday, as testified by the witness?"

CHIEF JUSTICE: "It is so noted."

HAFEZ: "With the honorable court's permission, in the interest of justice, I would like to grant the witness an opportunity to review his testimony so that he may correct any human errors due to a lapse of memory."

CHIEF JUSTICE: "Proceed."

HAFEZ: "Mr. Fredericks, you have testified that the phone call in question was received on a Thursday, in your presence. Is it possible you may have been mistaken?"

FREDERICKS: "Definitely not. It's all on the tape."

HAFEZ: "I was referring to the day, not to the nature of the call."

FREDERICKS: "Well . . . I'm pretty sure it was Thursday."

HAFEZ: "But you're not certain."

FREDERICKS: "It . . . it happened so long ago."

HAFEZ: "You remember the day the U.N. was destroyed, don't you?"

FREDERICKS: "Yes."

HAFEZ: "It was on a Friday. If the call came in the night before, you would have remembered that, wouldn't you? *In fact, you testified that you tried to apprehend Mr. Ring immediately after the phone call. Did you not?*"

*No answer.*

HAFEZ: "For the record, Mr. Fredericks, and to correct errors in memory, and to save the director of the prestigious FBI the humiliation and embarrassment of suffering a charge of perjury, I ask you: Didn't the call from Major Benn Yussid come in on Monday, four days before the destruction of the U.N.?"

*No answer. Facial muscles working. Dry mouth. Eyes darting.*

HAFEZ: "Does it matter what day the call came in, Mr. Fredericks? The tape in evidence tells the story. *Hard evidence, according to the tape, that David Ring conspired with the state of Israel to destroy the U.N. Building!* . . . Why perjure yourself over a date? When was it, Mr. Fredericks? Set the record straight. *Was it Monday or Thursday?*"

FREDERICKS: "*Monday! Monday night was when that call came in! When the plan was made to blow up the U.N.! Monday! You've got it there on that paper. That'll prove the call was made Monday night and that I'm telling the truth about the tape and the conspiracy. The tape, that's the best evidence. It's all there. Word for word.*"

HAFEZ: "Yes. Word for word. The tape in your hands outlining the conspiracy to destroy the U.N. Building, and *you did nothing to stop it! You had four days to place David Ring under arrest. To close his building. To postpone Sivad's visit until all was clear. To notify the world of the alleged plot. Instead you waited until the destruction was complete before you made your move. Tell this honorable court why you stood by and permitted thousands of human beings to be murdered. . . . honorable sirs, I submit that this witness, together with those humanoids seated there disguised as men, swastikas engraved on their foreheads, Klaus Wagner, Senator Franklyn, General Marley, Secretary Brandon and Reverend Carson, arranged and conspired to destroy the U.N. at the precise time of Yassim Sivad's visit so as to place the blame on David Ring as agent of Israel so as to provoke the world and thus give the conspirators a clear field for world domination. What other reason was there for Mr. Fredericks to permit the destruction? I submit that if this honorable court finds the defendant guilty as charged, then this witness is likewise guilty!"*

It was five full minutes before the hall quieted down. The chief justice gazed sternly at Hafez. "I will not permit you to usurp my judgment. I am fully aware of the implication of Mr. Fredericks' non-feasance. However, the tape revealing Mr. Ring's complicity in the U.N.'s destruction is still in evidence. Now I am ready to accept the telephone document into evidence."

Hafez smiled. "At no time, honorable sir, did I say I had such a document." He tore up the paper he'd been holding. "It's just . . . nothing. All I have is the sworn statement of the witness that the call was monitored on a Monday and not on a Thursday. If I have misled the court I humbly apologize."

The face of the chief justice tightened as he turned to the attorney general. "Do you wish to redirect?"

"The prosecution rests, honorable sir."

The chief justice raised his gavel. "There will be a recess for two hours."

He brought the gavel down.

# 35

The jeeps were stopped at the gate of the Syrian air force base in Damascus. Major Benn Yussid, dressed as an air force colonel, showed his papers and asked to be directed to the commandant.

The guard, with extreme deference, passed them through, then phoned General Faseer of their coming.

Benn Yussid's papers informed the commandant that he was Colonel Abu Ali, and that a helicopter gun-ship was to be placed at his command.

"We have information, general," said Yussid, "that the Israelis may attempt to rescue David Ring immediately after the trial. President Dasat has ordered me to transport him to Mezza Prison as soon as the court has rendered its judgment."

The general was a tall man with a small head and

piercing black eyes. He stared at Benn Yussid for a moment then signed the order.

The jeeps moved swiftly to the field where the helicopter was being made ready for takeoff.

The men abandoned the jeeps and piled into the waiting craft. Benn Yussid sat at the controls. He knew the ship; a Russian model, many of them captured during the Six-Day War. Benn Yussid had been a pilot then.

The huge chopper leaped into the air with a great thrashing of its blades.

General Faseer pressed the lever of his intercommunicator and told his aide: "Find out what you can about a Colonel Abu Ali out of Aleppo. Advise me as soon as you have the information."

He closed his eyes. Where had he seen this man before? His manner, his Arabic accent, so familiar. Abu Ali . . . Abu Ali . . . it wasn't the name. The name meant nothing. What was it? Not just his manner or accent. His eyes? Like ice. "The man's blood must be just above freezing," he muttered.

A shiver shook his frame.

The guards brought David back into the great hall of justice, removed his shackles and took up their positions, waiting for the court to reconvene.

Hafez came in and sat down beside him; his eyes betraying his anxiety.

David stared sightlessly. Thoughts of Myrna and her demise crowded his brain. The news had reached him through Hafez. The destruction of the B-52 was sabotage, they said. The Jews had done it. To get at the president. "*Also on board was the United States attorney general and his secretary Myrna Lu,*" was the way the story read.

There it was. All his people gone. It was only fitting

that he should go too. He felt Hafez' gaze; saw the concern in his eyes.

David turned. "It's over," he said. "Or it will be in an hour from now. I've no desire to go on, Hafez. I'll just lay out the facts." He gave him a wan smile. "At least you showed up Fredericks for the bastard he is."

"You've got to fight, David."

"I have none left in me."

"They claim an outrage. It can't match yours, David."

"It can if they believe I destroyed the U.N. and the thousands in and around it. And they do believe."

"What about Marley—Klaus Wagner, and the rest?"

"Names."

"Yes. But symbols of an abyss of deceit. You can't let them go on."

"I can't stop them."

The huge helicopter gunship circled the square, then began to descend, its rotors beating noisily at the air.

The people crowding the area scurried out of range of the sound and wind.

Slowly it settled, the noise deafening, dropping by degrees, blowing dust as it gingerly touched down. The big rotors slowed, drooped and died into silence.

The soldiers piled out, their automatic weapons at the ready. Led by Major Benn Yussid, they marched to the entrance doors of the great hall. "Special unit," he told the guards. "Report back to your base."

Four men took up their positions at the doors.

Eight entered the vast chamber where four soldiers guarded the exits. Benn Yussid relieved them with four of his own.

The remaining four moved quickly to the defendant's council table and replaced the four soldiers guarding David. At that moment the seven justices entered the dais and the people rose and Benn Yussid stood facing them, his back to David.

It was when the court came to order that Yussid turned and offered David a flash of a grin. Almost subliminal.

David's eyes went wide. Silently he mouthed: Benn Yussid. He glanced at the other guards. Did he detect a wink? His mind filled with hope. Maybe there was still time for the world to know. Unfettered, alive, with God's help he could maybe—maybe—find a way to bring the truth into the light. If . . .

"Honorable sirs . . ." Hafez' voice interrupted his thoughts. Hafez had never met Benn Yussid. ". . . at this time, I renew my request for expert witnesses to testify as to the validity of the tape in evidence."

"Denied."

"Then with your permission, Mr. Ring would like to address the court without being questioned by me. Of course, he will be subject to cross-examination."

"Permission granted."

"Take the ball, David," whispered Hafez solemnly. "Like when we were kids."

David nodded and went to the dock.

"Honorable sirs," he began. Then he looked into the eyes of the cameras. "People of the world, I hereby swear to tell the truth, completely and totally, before God."

His face darkened. "I am innocent of the crime referred to in the indictment; innocent of its commission, its contemplation, either consciously or subconsciously, in mind, in heart, in soul, in my bodily reflexes."

He turned to the chief justice. "At the outset, let

me remind the honorable court that the only hard evidence against me is the tape. If Mr. Fredericks had confessed that the tape was a fraud, then the court would have no alternative but to declare me innocent of the crimes charged. Since he has testified that the tape is authentic, in the interest of justice should I not be given an opportunity to question its validity?"

His voice quiet, yet heard through every corner of the vast hall. "Honorable sir, I humbly request that you reconsider your previous decision."

"Denied."

David turned to the cameras. "Then I offer my plea to the world! To President Dasat, who has appointed this jurist. To the jurists all over the world within range of my voice. *I submit that this court is biased, prejudiced, unfit to sit as a tribunal!*"

Silence. A deathly stillness.

The chief justice, his face livid, gazed down from his height.

"How dare you!"

David fired back. "I dare because my life hangs in the balance! I dare because the fate of the world rests on that piece of tape! I dare because if that tape proves fraudulent it will reveal a conspiracy of world destruction and enslavement of such proportion that the holocaust at the U.N. will appear to be just a minuscule conflagration in comparison.

"Since you deny a *humble request* for expert testimony, I *demand* that you procure scientific engineers and technicians from universities around the world to examine the tape. If they prove to your satisfaction that the tape is made up of bits and pieces strung together so as to give it a semblance of legitimacy, then I would demand that Carl Fredericks, together with the Klaus Wagner group, be tried before a world court for murder and conspiracy—a conspiracy threatening a world takeover.

"Should the expert testimony reflect that the tape is genuine, then the court will have had the profound satisfaction of proving to the world that it is a just court. I'm sure the court would not hesitate to accept such designation. And what would the opinion of the world be if the court denied me the opportunity to prove me innocent? The answer is quite obvious. As it is, your *dicta* of judicial notice on expert testimony in which you categorized it as 'an abuse of time,' will go down in the law books as the most asinine declaration ever made by a jurist." David smiled. "For that statement I could be held in contempt. But I wonder when, before or after the firing squad." Abruptly: "I hereby request the court to grant my demands."

"Denied," spoke the chief justice between clenched teeth.

David turned to the attorney general. "You may cross-examine."

"No questions."

"In that event, the defense rests."

The chief justice gazed about the great hall and announced: "The spectators will remain seated while the court weighs its judgment. Whatever it may be, you are not to leave until the defendant is removed."

The seven judges rose and retired to the chamber.

The aide knocked at General Faseer's door and entered. "I have the report you requested, sir," he said "on Colonel Abu Ali."

"Yes?"

"Shall I read from my notes, sir, or would you prefer a written draft?"

"Never mind, just tell me what you have," said the general testily.

The aide referred to his notes. "Abu Ali was with the Fifth Air Corps during the '67 war. Decorated for bravery. Credited with downing six Israeli planes . . ."

"Mmmmmm."

"Served as the president's personal pilot for three years . . ."

The general nodded, impressed.

"Resigned from the Air Force to head an intelligence unit. Reactivated during the Yom Kippur War and again decorated." He looked up. "That's about it, sir."

"Thank you. I can't remember having met him before. But he looked most familiar."

"Yes, sir."

"That will be all."

"*Yes . . . sir!*" He saluted smartly, wheeled and started for the door, then paused, turned. . . . "Excuse me, sir."

"Yes?"

"I forgot to mention . . ."

The general scowled.

"Colonel Abu Ali died in an Israeli prison camp."

The general lurched for the phone.

The judges were still deliberating. Hafez thought it was a good sign.

"I don't trust the chief justice," said David.

"He has only one vote."

"An important one."

It was then David made known Benn Yussid's presence. He whispered. "If it goes against me, come with us."

Hafez shook his head. "Better that I work for you from this end."

David caught Benn Yussid's nod.

A knock was heard at the chamber door. The bailiff announced: "All rise."

The judges filed in and took their seats. The chief justice sounded his gavel as a signal for the spectators to be seated.

"The defendant will please rise," intoned the chief justice.

David stood tall and straight.

"David Ring, you will be interested to learn that it is the unanimous opinion of this court that Carl Fredericks is guilty of nonfeasance in his duty as Chief of the FBI. Obviously he is beyond our jurisdiction. The onus rests with your government to deal with him as it chooses. I am certain the proper authorities will study the case thoroughly and justice will be done."

David laughed derisively.

The chief justice, disconcerted, continued. "As to the charges against you, the court is divided in its judgment. Justices Nakhel, Fasil and Ilyad voted for acquittal. Justices Muzi, Baida and Fawzi voted for conviction. It therefore becomes my burden to cast the deciding vote."

The great hall was still except for the sound of a mass intake of breath.

The chief justice adjusted his glasses and cleared his throat. "I quote from Chapter Thirty-five of the Koran." He read: " 'If God should punish men according to what they deserve, he would not leave on the back of the earth so much as a beast.' "

He looked up. "Justice here is meted out not according to what men deserve but what the law demands. One may not *demand* justice. One may only *demand* that he not suffer an injustice." He pointed a finger. "David Ring, you are charged with a heinous crime. But you need not fear an injustice from me, though you have accused me of bias and prejudice.

In my view the law demands that you be punished. Provided you are found guilty."

Again the chief justice adjusted his glasses and cleared his throat. He read: "David Ring, I hereby find you guilty as charged."

A mutter rose from the throats of the hundreds of people.

The gavel came down.

"Does the defendant wish to speak before I pronounce sentence?"

"Yes." Now David pointed a finger. "Tell the people of the world—the cameras are on you—*who gave you jurisdiction over me*. By what right have you taken it upon yourselves to try me for an alleged crime that took place in the United States, where people from every nation in the world were killed? By what right did you supersede the rights of other nations to try me, such as England, France, Belgium, China, the Netherlands, Norway, Sweden . . . shall I name all of them?

"How dare you sit there in your sanctimony and point a finger of doom at me who was brought here at the point of a gun and not permitted an opportunity to prove the tape that convicted me was a sham.

"I thank God the world is witness to your injustice. Allah must be ashamed."

He turned away and sat down.

The voice of the chief justice trembled as he pronounced: "You will die by firing squad at sunset one week from today."

A roar of protest rose from the crowd. Louder than thunder. Like the sound of an avalanche.

"No! No! No!"

Fists were upraised. Women wept.

"No! No! No!"

David whispered to Benn Yussid then embraced

Hafez wordlessly. The guards hustled him out a side door.

Benn Yussid leaped over the guard railing to the clerk who sat trembling. "Give me the tape before they destroy it."

The clerk was glad to get rid of it.

Outside, the helicopter's rotor blades were in action. David climbed in with the raiders as Benn Yussid came racing across the square to the ship and swung himself up into the cockpit. He veered the huge craft across the square, then straight up and away.

Speaking Hebrew, Benn Yussid radioed Tel Aviv their position and the expected time of arrival.

The Mig 21's swooped down out of the cloud cover and buzzed around the helicopter like wasps.

The speaker on Benn Yussid's radio crackled: *"Follow us or we'll blow you out of the sky."*

Benn Yussid held his course. "Who are you?" he replied to the threat. He needed time. He was outgunned.

*"Turn due west. At once."*

He began his turn slowly and at the same time started his craft into a climb.

*"Level off!"*

"I'm having trouble. I'm not used to this ship."

He continued to climb.

*"Level off! Level off!"*

"The controls are jammed."

David looked out. Would they make the cloud cover?

The shot crossed the ship's bow. *"Last warning. Level off and head due west."*

Benn Yussid looked at David and shrugged. "You win some, you lose some. Do we go to the Damascus Air Force Base?"

"It would be nice," said David with a sigh, "if the cavalry showed up."

Benn Yussid peered out the Plexiglas bubble. "Funny you should mention it."

The Phantoms with the Star of David on their fuselages came in at a beautiful angle so as to be seen instantly by the Migs.

The Migs refused the challenge.

They headed due west for their base.

"Shalom!" said a voice from one of the Phantom radios.

The government of Israel received word that unless David Ring was returned to Damascus within forty-eight hours, the Arab nations, with the active support of the Soviet Union, would commence an invasion.

A lot of things could happen in forty-eight hours. Like world conflagration.

# 36

## Lake George, N.Y.

Ralph Hobson sat at a small desk in the bare office of the Lake George Motel. He was in shirtsleeves. The bright afternoon sun bouncing off the white walls accented the ghastly pallor of Ralph Hobson's face. Light blue veins pressing against skin that seemed to be wearing thin crisscrossed along his hands, arms, neck, and temples. There was barely enough flesh on his body to protect his bones. He appeared to be a very sick man.

The tendons on the side of his temples twitched nervously as he regarded the reel of tape on his desk. It seemed so long ago that he'd transcribed it from the original, the time when that woman played it in the adjoining room. He remembered how he had trembled when he first listened to it. Now he was trembling again. What he had here could change the course of history.

He hadn't meant to tell Henry Ackermann, the cell leader, that the cassette was blank. It had just . . . come out. He had placed the transcribed tape in his safe deposit box. And it had remained there. Until today.

Ralph Hobson had watched the trial of David Ring on television from start to finish. What frightened him was that Henry Ackermann might have watched it too, and would know by now that the cassette wasn't a blank. Then again maybe he hadn't watched the whole thing. Maybe he had missed the part about the cassette. Sure. Otherwise Hobson would have heard from him. But there had been nothing. He had to know. He dialed Ackermann's number.

"Hello, Henry. Ralph. That was a hell of a trial, wasn't it? . . . Did you see the whole thing? . . . I heard over the radio that Ring escaped to Israel. . . . Yeah, Dasat gave them forty-eight hours then goodbye Yids. . . . Listen, Henry, I gotta run down to New York for a couple of days to see my nephew. Pretty sick. Anything I can do for you while I'm there? . . . Okay, just thought I'd tell you. So long."

He replaced the phone and emitted a sigh of relief. He carefully wrapped the tape in plastic, went to his room to pack a bag.

He withdrew two thousand dollars from the bank. Enough to see him through.

At the bar in the airport, he stared into his drink, deep in thought.

*The tape should be worth a million dollars to David Ring.*

*And another million from the Israeli government.*

The Israeli cabinet was in emergency session. Forty-eight hours to perdition. To give up David Ring was out of the question. Yet, was it not wiser to sacrifice one man for the benefit of many?

*Total mobilization of every man, woman and child. A nation with a single heartbeat. Enslavement, never! They would release the bomb. So agreed.*

David stood at the council table and shook his head. "Mr. Prime Minister," he said. "Call President Dasat and tell him I'm prepared to give myself up immediately. Not as a prisoner to stand before a firing squad, but as your emissary. Tell him that the tape has been forwarded to London where it will be examined by electronic scientists of ten nations. Including the Soviet Union. They'll need two weeks to file their conclusions. During that time the armies will remain static.

"Should the report prove the tape authentic . . ." He paused, and gazed soberly at the group. ". . . then I die and Israel surrenders."

Pandemonium.

David waited until the clamor subsided.

"Do you think the tape is authentic?" he said softly, surveying the group.

Major Benn Yussid grinned. "If so, then you are accusing me of treason."

Silence.

The prime minister got up from his chair. "I will make the call," he said.

An unarmed Israeli plane landed at the Damascus airport where it was met by President Dasat.

David Ring disembarked and was escorted by the president to his residence. To be placed under house arrest. Until the result of the tests on the tape were known.

At the same time Jerusalem received a call from London.

*A bomb exploded in an electronic laboratory.*
*The building was destroyed.*
*Including the tape.*
Klaus Wagner and his fellow conspirators sat at a bar in Damascus and toasted each other.

# 37

## New York City

Ralph Hobson checked into the Americana Hotel under the name: Ralph Burns, Oswego, New York.

When the bellman put his suitcase on the rack, he told him to send up a fifth of Johnny Walker, black. He tipped him grandly.

He removed his jacket and hung it up neatly in the wardrobe.

In the drawer of the night table alongside the bed he found a phone book. He called the Passport Bureau in the Federal Building. He planned to book a flight to Amsterdam. From there he would be able to get through to Israel.

They told him it would take ten days for a passport.

He frowned. Ten days would be too late. David

Ring would be gone in ten days. So would the state of Israel. So would his two million dollars.

*The Dutch consul general! Holland was sympathetic!*

He called and made an appointment for the morning.

*Good.*

The bellman knocked, then entered with the bottle. "Will there be anything else, sir?" he asked.

On an impulse, he blurted, "How about . . . a woman? A young woman." He was embarrassed saying it.

"It'll cost you a C-note. Plus ten percent for me."

Ralph Hobson opened his wallet and handed him the money.

"In a half hour," said the bellman.

He had finished a quarter of the bottle when the door buzzer sounded.

She was young. No more than eighteen. What a body! His heart quickened when she stepped out of her dress. He felt his breath whistling. It had been such a long time . . .

She knew her business. "I'm going to undress you," she said, her voice barely above a whisper.

He stood trembling as she slowly, carefully, began removing his clothing, all the while whimpering as if she were getting a charge out of it.

She had him naked and he reached out for her.

"Not yet, baby," she said in a hushed tone. "Don't move." She ran her fingers lightly across his thin frame, guttural noises now emerging from her throat.

"Please . . ." he said. His heart was pounding wildly. "It's unbearable."

"Don't speak," she whispered. "Kathy has a surprise for you."

Her fingers continued to explore, eyes closed, mouth slack. Her nails left a trail down his chest to his stomach while his face flamed. Suddenly, she dropped to her knees and found him.

He screamed.

And died.

## *Damascus, Syria*

Damascus received word from the Soviet Union that the tape in the electronic laboratory had been destroyed. The Soviets suggested that the bomb was set by Israelis since it had been a foregone conclusion that the scientists would have found the tape to be authentic. A demand: the sentence against David Ring be carried out.

*David learned of the explosion before the government. Benn Yussid had phoned the story to him.*

And he knew what had to be done.

Two men guarded his room. The room was large, had a high ceiling and two double casement windows three stories above the ground.

David opened the left casement quietly, peering out from behind the drapes.

The roof was slate. Slippery. It had a wide gutter that led to a drainpipe. Might help.

Directly beneath, on the second floor, were two small balconies that probably led to two bedrooms.

Curving away from the area beneath his windows was a wide gravel path that disappeared into the darkness and the trees. But there were men on guard.

He looked at his watch. It was nearly ten o'clock. Soon his hosts would learn of the explosion in the London laboratory. He knew that his house arrest would come to an end and he would be placed in a cell to await execution.

David eased himself out of the window, holding on to the sill until his feet touched the gutter. He side-stepped his way along the roof toward the drainpipe only a few feet away.

He lowered his body cautiously against the roof; he reached out, gripped the gutter on the far side of the drainpipe with his right hand, and slowly, carefully, crouched sideways, inching his feet into a support position. He pushed against the outside rim of the gutter, testing its strength, and in a quick, springing, short jump, he leaped over the side, holding the rim with both hands, his feet against the wall, straddling the drainpipe.

He began his descent, hand-below-hand on the pipe.

Suddenly he heard a loud crashing above him. There were shouts in Arabic and the sounds of wood shattering.

Guards were breaking into his room.

*They had gotten the word.*

One of the balconies was parallel with him. He swung beneath it, his body dangling thirty feet above the ground but out of sight.

Men were at the windows above looking out, shouting to the guards below to fan out in search.

The shouts above David receded from the window, and he managed to swing back to the drainpipe.

He reached the ground and raced along the gravel path into the darkness of the trees.

*He didn't see the Doberman.*

The giant animal leaped at the target of human flesh. The teeth tore into David's arm.

David lashed at the dog with his free hand. He fell to the ground, wrenching, rolling, twisting his body. The monster held on, savage growls emanating from his throat.

David could get no leverage to use his hand.

*The Doberman's teeth below the shoulder . . .*

*Excruciating pain.*

*Then David felt the sharp pointed rock under his hand. He tried to hit the dog with it.*

*No leverage.*

*He had to get to his feet. The teeth had reached the bone.*

*The head kept whipping.*

*Now on his feet. The Doberman on his hind legs, gnashing at the bone.*

*David jabbed the sharp rock with all the strength he had into the soft stomach of the animal. Warm blood erupted from the dog's lacerated belly; the swallowed sound of a savage roar burst from the animal's throat as it died.*

David dropped on his back, gasping for air.

*A man held a rifle barrel to his head.*

# 38

## New York City

Captain Peter Hansen, Twenty-second Precinct, wept for his friend David Ring. The horrifying events beginning with the U.N. explosion filled him with a desperate fear. Not for himself, for the people. They were being led like sheep. And he knew they would be destroyed. As David was destroyed.

He sat in his office, mourning. He had followed the trial. A railroad job. And now they were going to take David's life.

He was furious. Where was the voice of the church?

Silence.

Where was God?

Silence.

Captain Peter Hansen opened a desk drawer and removed a pint bottle of rye and poured himself a stiff drink.

He continued to brood. The drink didn't help.

The policeman on duty entered the property room and handed the property master a suitcase. "Name of Ralph Burns," he said. "Died of a heart attack in the Americana. Comes from Oswego. There is no Ralph Burns in Oswego."

The property master entered the facts in a book.

The policeman turned in a large envelope. "Plenty of cash." He tore the envelope open and spilled out $1,726.27 on the counter. In addition to a gold ring, a tie clasp and an empty wallet without any I.D.

The policeman eyed the money longingly. "Too bad I'm honest."

"Too bad."

"How about you?"

"Likewise."

"Too bad."

The policeman left the room. The property master placed the money, the ring, and the tie clasp in the safe. Then he opened the suitcase and entered the contents in the ledger.

Two jackets.

Two pairs of slacks.

Two shirts.

Two pair underwear shorts.

Two pair underwear shirts.

Two pair socks.

One pair shoes. Brown.

He found the tape wrapped in plastic.

Blank?

Maybe not.

He stuck his head out the door. "Who's got a tape recorder?"

Someone answered: "The captain's got one."

He knocked at the captain's door and entered.

"This was in the effects of a deceased," he said. "I don't know if anything's on it."

"Why don't you try playing it?" growled Hansen.

"Yeah. Can I borrow your machine?"

Captain Hansen opened the bottom drawer of his desk and removed the recorder. "Watch out you don't press the record button by mistake. It'll wipe off anything that's on it."

"Why should I do that?"

"Do what?"

"Press the record button by mistake."

Hansen glared at him. "Because the record button doesn't say 'record button.' It doesn't say anything. And the playback button doesn't say anything either." His mood was bad.

"Which is the playback button?"

"The one on the right."

The property master took the machine to the property room. He placed it on the counter. He carefully threaded the tape to the receiving reel, giving it several turns by hand.

He eyed it for a moment. Which was the recording button?

On the right.

Yeah. On the right.

Then the playback must be on the left.

Can't be too careful.

He pressed the record button by mistake.

Nothing.

He pressed down hard.

The tape spun weakly for two revolutions then stopped.

The property master picked up the machine and took it back to Captain Hansen. "It doesn't work," he said. To prove it, he kept pressing the recording button.

Captain Hansen nearly screamed. "You goddamn idiot! You're lucky it doesn't work! You're pressing the record button!"

"Holy shit."

"Jesus!"

"It might have been a blank anyway."

"Sure." He pressed the playback. That didn't work. "Batteries must be dead."

There were batteries in the bottom drawer. He replaced the old ones.

"I'll take it back," said the property master.

"As long as it's threaded let's hear it." He pressed the playback button. The tape spun slowly. Too slowly. He raised the speed to 7½.

They heard only the surface noises as Myrna had. The captain looked at the property master and shrugged.

Then the sudden admixture of voices. Indistinguishable. Odd words . . . laughter. *Then the voice of Carl Fredericks . . .*

*"Gentlemen . . . Anna . . . may I present Klaus Wagner!"*

*It all spilled out.*

*The frame.*

*The conspiracy.*

The policemen listened in shock. The property master's jaw was open. Tears streamed down Captain Hansen's face. He wept unashamedly. His body in spasms of sobs.

And then it was finished.

Hansen moved his finger to the stop button, carefully.

Silence.

"Frank," said Hansen, his voice barely audible. "Sit there, Frank. Don't say a word. Don't move. You didn't hear anything. Remember that. If you breathe a word of it your life won't be worth a plugged nickel. Not a word. Not even in this precinct. Do you hear me, Frank?"

Frank nodded and swallowed.

"This town is filled with traitors. God knows how many! Oh, Lord Jesus Christ!"

He lifted the phone. "Lucy . . . Captain Hansen. Is there anybody there who can relieve you at the board for a minute? . . . Good. I want to see you."

He hung up. "Remember what I said, Frank." It was a whisper. "Not even to your wife."

The operator came in. "Lucy. I want you to do something for me. It'll be the most important thing you will ever have done in your whole life. Okay?"

She nodded, puzzled.

"Do you know any of the overseas operators? One you can trust?"

"Yeah. A very good friend of mine."

"You can trust her to keep her mouth shut, no matter what?"

"Yeah."

Hansen closed his eyes for a moment and breathed a prayer. "Place a call," he said "to Jerusalem, Israel. Person-to-person with either the prime minister or Major Benn Yussid."

She stood there staring.

"*Do it!*"

She whirled and dashed out of the door.

They sat in silence, the two of them. Hansen opened the desk drawer and got out his bottle of rye. And two shot glasses. He filled them. Without a word he pushed one over to Frank, whose face still wore the shock lines.

"Oh, heavenly father . . ." breathed Peter Hansen. It was a religious draining of the glasses.

They waited.

A clock on the wall ticked.

There was a knock at the door, a sergeant poked his head in. "Hey, captain . . ."

"Get the hell out!" screamed Hansen.

The door slammed shut, the frosted glass shivered. They waited.

Finally, Hansen broke the silence. "Funny thing. At a time like this, each minute goes by and it feels like an hour. I remember, the first time I made love to my wife. We were together for an hour. It felt like a minute." He paused, contemplating a cherished memory. "Is that maybe Einstein's theory of relativity?"

They laughed.

The tension was broken. And the phone rang.

It was the operator. She had them both on the line; the prime minister and Major Benn Yussid.

Captain Peter Hansen told them what he had.

# 39

## Damascus, Syria

The courtyard.

Twilight. The sun, what was left of it, brushed the sky in pastel pink trimmed with swirls of white clouds. A light breeze came up from the southeast, sending little eddies of dust in a *grand jeté*. Wraithlike.

Overlooking the yard was the room reserved for the witnesses to the execution. An enormous window faced the courtyard.

Present in the room were the military brass, the seven judges of the supreme court, selected news representatives from all over the world, heads of state and President Millah Dasat.

Seated with the president were Klaus Wagner, Carl Fredericks, Secretary Brandon, Senator Franklyn, Reverend Carson and General Marley. They hadn't wanted to stay; but President Dasat had insisted. It was their evidence that had brought about the conviction, explained Dasat. Their work in uncovering the great conspiracy. It was only proper that they bear witness to the result.

The room was silent.

Wagner shifted his muscular body in his chair and ran his fingers through his blond hair. General Marley, trying to fit his lanky frame in a chair too small for it, looked impatiently at his watch.

Reverend Carson sat bent and scowling, his small eyes watching the courtyard with an expression akin to hunger. Senator Franklyn sat erect, his curly hair seeming to bristle with anticipation, as though he were prepared to mount to some invisible podium and harangue another crowd.

Secretary of State Brandon sat stolidly in his seat, his small, fat body fitting neatly into its cushions, his schoolboy pout playing about his mouth as he seemed to contemplate some slight about to be inflicted upon him.

Fredericks, appearing thinner than ever and even more tense since his humiliation on the witness stand, gnawed intently on a hangnail.

All were anxious to get this over with and return to the States. There was much work to be done.

Dasat noticed their impatience. "Any minute now," he said in a reassuring tone.

"What's holding it up, Mr. President?" Marley asked.

"Oh . . . certain preparations," the president replied. "We do these things according to tradition."

"Hmmph."

Silence.

A scraping of a chair.

A cough.

Then a murmur of surprise.

David Ring entered the courtyard from a side gate. He was alone. One arm was in a full cast, held in place diagonally across his chest by a sheet of adhesive tape.

He stood against the far wall staring up at the window. He could see them all clearly. Especially Klaus Wagner and the conspirators.

They wondered where the firing squad was. Where were the soldiers? Marley tossed the president a questioning look.

Dasat smiled. "Patience," he said.

*"Klaus Wagner!"* It was David's voice heard through the loudspeaker, transmitted by the tiny microphone he wore. *"Listen! Carl Fredericks! Listen! Marley! Carson! Listen! Franklyn! Brandon! Listen!"*

Then came the voice from the tape. The tape Myrna had found. Anna Thornton's tape. Ralph Hobson's tape. Captain Hansen's tape.

*"He's here! Klaus Wagner!"* Carl Frederick's voice sounded from the loudspeakers.

*"Klaus, in this room you see the group that represents the supreme power, the authority, the control of the Nazi movement in America."*

Shock struck the conspirators into a deathly silence. They stared with expressions of terror and hate as the tape rolled on.

Klaus Wagner's voice: *. . . Yassim Sivad's presence, his words, his image will be televised and carried by satellite around the world. At which time the General Assembly Hall will be blown up. We will execute this deed in such a manner that the overwhelming evidence will point to David Ring as the contractor on behalf of the Jewish state.. . . .*

They sat motionless, frozen in fear. Sightless.

The Israeli prime minister entered the room quietly,

together with Major Benn Yussid, Captain Peter Hansen and Hafez Ameer.

The tape continued: . . . *The people will be ours! The United States of America will be ours. The rest of the world will fall in line. We have seven days! It shall be done!*

End of tape.

Klaus Wagner let out a horrible scream and fell thrashing to the floor in an epileptic fit.

The others ignored him.

The president of Syria turned to the Israeli prime minister.

"Do you want them? The animals rightly belong to you."

"Would you like to have them?" asked the prime minister.

"I think we would."

"They are yours."

Through the window they saw David raise his face to the sky and they heard his voice through the speaker. *"Sh'ma Yisrael, Adonai Elohaynu, Adonai Ehad!"* Hear O Israel! The Lord our God is one God!

David stood alone in the courtyard. And he thought of Myrna who died for him. And Al, and Harry, and Jonathan, who died for him. Yes, and even Lippy. And all those others.

Was there someone *he* could die for?

He saw Hafez and Pete Hansen running across the courtyard toward him.

Maybe . . .

In the deadly world of international espionage,
love is the total risk . . .

# THE HUMAN FACTOR

## GRAHAM GREENE

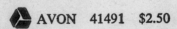 AVON   41491   $2.50

HF 5-79